Cafferty and Quinn are also featured in:

<u>Novels -</u>

Let the Dead Sleep,

Waking the Dead,

The Dead Play On (Novel Length,)

<u>Novellas</u>

Toys in the Attic,

Big Easy Evil, and

Blood on the Bayou (Novella length)

<u>Short Story,</u>

Infernal Night (co-written with F. Paul Wilson)

D1715345

BITTER RECKONING

Heather

Graham

For Kelsey, with love & thanks

Prologue

Ally

"Hallowed Angel Cemetery and Mount Misery. A couple of the eeriest places you'll ever see," the man driving Ally Caldwell said casually. He glanced her way, adding, "Especially around what we refer to as harvest time. They say the land was cursed from the time the natives came, and they were glad to leave it all to the Europeans. October always seemed especially harrowing here."

Ally thought she had hired a driver—not a tour guide. She should have known better when he hadn't opened the back door for her but had opened the front passenger's side of the sedan they would take, instead.

What the hell?

Fine, she hadn't cared where she sat. She was late and just wanted to get where she was going. But now...Ugh. She really had no patience for conversation—she was in the car for a ride, nothing more. Besides which, she didn't believe in eerie places, old legends, or anything of the like. She was on the way to a conference where her planned speech could mean the difference between a little bungalow just outside the city for her, or an elegant house in the French Quarter or Garden District.

Mount Misery and Hallowed Angel Cemetery might be creepy, eerie, or anything else—didn't matter. They had nothing to do with where she was going. Her destination was the Honeywell Lodge situated on a small but charming bayou to the northwest of New Orleans and southeast of the city of Lafayette.

Calling anything "Mount" here was a major exaggeration. But she understood; land fill in this area had created something that resembled a rise, if not a hill; and so, she supposed, they were welcome to call the area whatever they wanted. His conversation was jarring, however. She thought they were past Halloween—and all the nonsense that went with it—people jumping out here and there and thinking they were funny, and the motion-operated creatures that went off every damned time she walked down an aisle in a drug store. She didn't want this idiot talking about anything weird or creepy. It was over. She didn't even want to exert the energy to block him out.

She was just eager to reach her destination.

Ally hadn't been there yet, but she had seen pictures. The lodge was charming in every manner of the word. Every room was a suite, the restaurant offered gourmet food, and there was both an indoor and outdoor swimming pool. The place was so well cleaned and maintained that even the stables seemed to shine in the photos.

"You know," the driver continued—heedless of the fact she'd ignored his attempts at conversation so far, "lots of old cemeteries are now surrounded by civilization. Neighborhoods—businesses. They're in the light. I mean, look at St. Louis #1 back in the Big Easy. Right there off Rampart

Street—not that you can go there anymore without a guide. But it's there—surrounded by city. Lafayette Cemetery in NOLA—Commander's Palace is across the street, elegant homes, a wonderful book store. Nothing around Hallowed Angel Cemetery. On one side is the swamp! Marshland and sugar cane—miles and miles and miles of sugar cane. Really. There are just a few houses on the spits of solid ground around it. The entrance is way back off the Bayou Teche. Then to the right of it and down the road, there's a big warehouse for farm equipment, and most of the time no one is around."

He turned his head looking at her directly, hoping for a reaction.

She gave him none. Hopefully, that would make him quit talking.

Nope. He kept on anyway.

"The cemetery is filled with old, broken, decaying mausoleums, headless angels, cherubs, weird pyramid tombs, 'oven vaults,' and there's even a banshee riding a winged horse in a section where some Irish were interred. A bunch of Civil War soldiers—both North and South—got thrown into a big tomb together. By the time crews got to the dead, lots of bugs and stuff had been at work, and they weren't even sure who the tell-tale belt-buckles and all had gone to!" He paused to grin. "Sometimes, there are even bones sticking out when the old tombs get broken. Oh, so much more—it's overgrown—funny, like they say about New Orleans often enough—it's pure decaying elegance and creepiness. If you go to Hallowed Angel at night, it's dark—and worse on nights when the moon is full—

shadows are everywhere. Or of course, Cursed Yvette is running around with her light. Then again," he added cheerfully, "that made the land for *Honeywell Lodge* incredibly reasonable when Colleen wanted to invest in another place!" He grinned at her, waiting for a reply—some comment of fear or horror. "And the resort is on good land. It was planned for some kind of a research center, and the idea got canned by budget cuts, but a lot of landfill was already there so it's great property."

He looked at her again hoping for a response.

Ally was not going to give in to him. The man was in his early thirties. She had never met him before—she'd just been promised a driver. But he was probably one of the brown-butts, trying to climb the ranks within Colleen's upstart company, Rankin Enterprises. She had originally formed it as just a dating site, but she'd been so successful that her company had grown unbelievably through her visions—and belief.

Colleen Rankin...Ally's boss.

Ally sighed inwardly.

Colleen was still—rather ridiculously, in Ally's mind—a big believer in romance and all things romantic. To be fair, Colleen had begun her dating site—Let's Meet—with a pure and loving heart, never ripping anyone off for the pleasure of meeting someone else. But meetings could be awkward, so when Colleen's father had passed away leaving her some seed money, she'd opened her first location, *Meet Me Face to Face,* seven years ago. By sheer luck, Ally was certain, Colleen had secured beachfront property in the Florida panhandle. There had been an old beat-up motor hotel on the property, and Colleen had it redone with a concentration on public areas that allowed for mingling—and a few private areas within the space for more personal conversations. The hotel was small, just seventy-five rooms, and she had welcomed guests herself for the first year and arranged for special parties which she also attended.

After *Meet Me Face to Face,* Colleen had built *Coffee and Conversation* in North Carolina. Again, she had worked there herself, setting the tone and the standard.

Now, they were heading to *Honeywell Lodge,* Colleen's newest resort just two hours outside of New Orleans, Louisiana, and while she hadn't seen it yet, Ally had been a part of all the planning, and many of her ideas had been embraced.

As much as she had come to hate Halloween, she was the one who had suggested opening and having a massive "Harvest Costume Ball" to celebrate the opening.

With the success of the other operations and Colleen's pleasure with Ally's ideas and successful marketing plans, Ally was ready to pitch her idea for the Caribbean. It was a place she was certain that could rise above anything thus far in Colleen's imagination—or of any of the other idea people and designers in the company.

"There, look, there's the entrance to the cemetery!" the driver pointed out.

It wasn't unusual to see nothing but miles and miles of green land, bayou, and marsh once the big city was left behind in Louisiana, but it seemed, having turned off Highway 90, they were cruising no-man's land. They were now officially in the middle of nowhere. She knew the area had been settled by the French and the French Canadians and still retained much of its

"Cajun" personae; but when the Spanish had ruled Louisiana, they had also left their stamp. Then the English had come and also the Americans, Italians, Portuguese, and more; but it retained a flavor of Cajun country; something that worked for Colleen since her mother had been born in Broussard, Louisiana.

They filmed a few ridiculous reality shows out in this area—guys without teeth chasing alligators, swamp people living in muck, and other such annoying fare. Ally wasn't from here, but she had been out on a site inspection and she knew if she were from here, she'd be royally ticked off. She'd met a fair amount of people. They'd all had their teeth.

As hard as she'd worked to ignore her driver, she couldn't help looking up as they reached the ridiculously named cemetery. Which, of course, allowed him to believe his playful attempts at spooking her had credence. A crumbling old stone wall surrounded the cemetery, but it was, at its highest points here and there, barely two-and-a-half-feet high. Still, massive iron gates with a stone arch announced the entry, leading to an overgrown road that apparently twisted through acreage of the dead—memorialized with crumbling stones, above-ground sarcophagi, mausoleums, vaults, headless cherubs and wingless angels. The driver had slowed the car, so they could see.

He wasn't hampering anyone by barely moving his vehicle. There wasn't a car anywhere around them.

Ally had no interest in slowing down for any kind of a cemetery. She was about to speak, but the driver beat her to it.

"Look!" he said suddenly.

She couldn't help it, she looked in the direction of the cemetery and saw a little light was sparking here and there in the cemetery—as if a small flashlight had been tied to a cat's tail. As the light moved, it illuminated bits and pieces of the old cemetery—broken statuary, a half-crushed tomb, broken stones surrounded by weeds growing amok along the barely discernible trails throughout.

"Lights," Ally said flatly. She checked her reflection in her compact mirror. Still looking good. She was nearly forty-five but could pass for a good ten years younger. She had been blessed with rich, almost black hair—only touched up a bit at the roots now—and luminous green eyes. She was attractive and knew two things—one, she had to be ruthless as a woman in business; and of course, two, she had to know how to play it all very sweetly when necessary. Attractiveness was a boon. A cold heart was a necessity. Business was a game.

A game she knew how to play.

This weekend was important. She was something of a goddess, her driver was barely worth her notice, and he wasn't going to get her with his silly stories.

"Cursed Yvette!" he said, stopping the car by the gates.

"Oh, God," she murmured, saying the words aloud in annoyance.

She didn't hinder him in the least.

"There are many tales, and then again, it seems around here, many unfortunate women happened to be named Yvette. Anyway, one of the legends has it there was a farm house near here and a Cajun girl fell in love with an English boy. The family wouldn't have it—the whole affair had shadows of Romeo and Juliet. Yvette taught religious classes and the children loved her, but her English lover's parents wanted nothing of her. He finally caved and told her he'd never be with her. But he couldn't stand it and went back to her. When his mother discovered the truth she went, found Yvette, dragged her out to this cemetery and killed her—stabbing her to death. Right at harvest time, no less, during Martinmas!"

He paused for a minute, waiting to see if she'd ask about Martinmas. She knew what it meant—it was a French festival for St. Martin. They had built their ball around it.

Nope. Still not talking to him.

Didn't bother the man in the least.

"You know, around these parts it's not just Martinmas—it's a whole two-week period where everything revolves around the harvest." He made a face. "Mostly sugarcane in these parts; but it's still very cultural, French first, and then, of course, harvest festivals went on all over Europe."

There was no way she was going to feed into him; she remained silent.

He continued with, "So—stories! Yvette was then supposedly buried on the spot where the evil deed was perpetrated, hidden for all time, or so her killer—her lover's vengeful mother—thought. The villagers believed Yvette left because she couldn't bear losing her English love and had gone on to find a good Cajun boy somewhere. Then, just a year later her one-time lover's mother was found in the cemetery, stabbed to death and left tied up on a pole like a scarecrow. She was found all bloody and broken—her head bashed in, too.

Halloween week again, no less! She was found above dug-up ground, and in that ground, they found the bones of poor Yvette. Of course, deep down, Yvette's mother had always known the truth, and wasn't about to let her daughter's murder go ignored. She was half Irish—those Irish came up with that whole Jack-o-lantern thing, you know—and she also had Haitian blood, which meant she had the whole voodoo thing going on, too. So now, it's said around here, scarecrows come to life, and you can still hear Yvette crying out in the night! And..."

He paused, grinning at her.

"And?" As soon as she spoke, Ally could have kicked herself. She was encouraging him!

"Through the decades—the centuries, even —ever since then, every now and then a bitchy woman is found dead in the cemetery. Always right around Martinmas."

"Let's see. You're saying I'm a bitchy woman—"

"Never!" he assured her.

"—and," she continued, "fate has decreed women like me wind up dead here."

"No!" he said with horror. "No, I would never call you a bitch—or suggest in any way you should wind up dead here!"

She sighed. They were so close now to her destination. If only he'd shut up and drive!

If she wasn't so anxious or so irritated, she would have told him that though she might not hail from the area, if something was going to run around and create havoc all over, it would be a *rougarou,* or the local form of a werewolf, and not a screaming woman or a scarecrow.

But she didn't want to have a conversation. She didn't want to feed into him in any way.

"You know, you can call me anything you want. But can we just go—"

She broke off as he frowned suddenly, jerking to the side of the road—right in front of the rusting cemetery arches—and cutting the car's engine.

"What are you doing?" Ally demanded. "Seriously. This is getting old, boring—and damned wearisome. Let's go."

"No, no—did you hear that? Someone was screaming."

"Don't be ridiculous," Ally said, but then she paused, wincing. Yes, someone was screaming, and the sound seemed to be coming from the heart of the cemetery.

"It's just kids!" she said. "Kids playing around—because it is a spooky old cemetery."

The scream kept sounding, as if someone was terrified or in agony.

"I'll be right back," he said, staring at her as if she were made of ice—or maybe rethinking his bitch opinion. He reached into the glove compartment for a flashlight as he added, "I can't ignore that—it's a cry for help!"

Then he was gone, the driver's door slamming in his wake. Ally stared after him in surprise.

He pushed at the old arching ironwork gates and disappeared, racing down one of the overgrown paths and behind an old oak, heavy-laden with branches and growing right through a worn tombstone.

Ally let out a deep sigh of aggravation and pulled out her cell phone, checking her email messages.

She had a long missive from Colleen who was very happy. Many of her singles and couples had arrived early. They were enjoying the pools and spas, the little "cinemas" she'd set up, the cabanas, the restaurants, and the clubs. Colleen couldn't wait for her to see how well it was going.

Ally had missed the first mixer—which was happening now and was just about over. Well, she'd had work to do. But Colleen had texted her from the event and she was happy about her mixer—it had gone off just about over.

And here she was, staring at cemetery gates.

"Right!" Ally muttered aloud. "Yep, they'll all get together. Some will get lucky, some will get mad...but, go figure. Maybe just getting lucky is what people want."

She had a few other emails. She read them, then turned to look back toward the cemetery.

Where the hell is that driver? Surely, he could have saved the fucking world by now.

It had been late when they left New Orleans. The greenery seemed to be very dark in color. All the world around her seemed darker still. One thing her loquacious driver had said was true, though. Where they were...it was damned dark. The moon shed some weak light. The only other light came from the beams at the front of their rental car. It was just dark.

The darkness intensified as she had sat there, but she'd been reading emails on her phone, and...

The moon really didn't help much. It seemed to cast a gray glow over the entire decaying spit of land that held the weed-laden cemetery with its chipped and broken everything.

"Come on, where are you—asshole!" she said aloud, looking around for her driver.

Irritated, she got out of the car. Surely, someone else had to be headed to the resort, someone who would have to pass by this road. She would hitch a ride.

She waited. She watched the darkness seem to grow deeper still.

She wasn't afraid of cemeteries—dead people couldn't hurt her—nor did the decaying statuary and weeds or the forlorn appearance of the place scare her.

The problem was, the color of the night was annoying; the yellowish glow of the moon created a strange green-gray cast that seemed to cause bizarre shadows to sweep around tombs, tombstones, broken angels and more.

The dead, she reminded herself, were the safest people on earth.

It was the living ones who could be dangerous.

As she stood there waiting—and waiting—she began to see faces in the shadows. She cursed at herself—she was not going to be frightened.

There had been no more screams, but neither had her driver reappeared or anyone else for that matter.

Someone...someone would come.

Someone did.

A beat-up old truck came sliding up alongside the sedan. She shielded her eyes from the headlamps. Once her eyes adjusted, she saw, to her great disappointment, the man at the wheel appeared to be...filthy. Cruddy, filthy—an old drunk, maybe! He had a thin wrinkled face, and a long graying beard that surely held crumbs from his last ten meals.

Disgusting.

He was the kind of person they made those bad reality shows about—he probably had no teeth.

He leaned toward his open window. "Hey, girlie, you want a ride?" he shouted out.

"No. I'm waiting," she said flatly.

"You sure you're good here? Weird things happen in these parts," he warned, shaking his head. "Some beau leave you just standing here while he went off exploring? It's all right—I'll give you a ride," he said.

She wasn't particularly rude—most of the time. It didn't make good business sense. But now she was anxious, impatient, and growing furious. She could admit it, she hadn't really cared what her driver had found, until she realized he couldn't have discovered anyone in real distress, because if he had, he'd have called for an ambulance or the police, and by now there would be someone...bathed...out here, asking if she needed a ride!

"I'm fine!" she snapped, waving a hand in the air.

He shrugged, but then she saw the truck moving forward and pulling off the road as well!

She wasn't afraid of danger; she was afraid of vomiting if the man touched her. So she did the only thing she could think of, she turned and headed into the cemetery, shouting for her driver.

There was no answer; she hurried in. As she did so, she could hear the disgusting bearded man grumble. "Hey, lady, I was just trying to help!"

Ally followed one of the overgrown trails and walked by several of the above ground single tombs or single sarcophagi— whatever they called those above ground enclosures—and to what she thought was the side of the trail, a place where a gnarled old oak was growing right through a tombstone.

Suddenly, she saw the light.

Light. That had to mean her driver.

She couldn't help herself; she started walking toward it, and now she was shaking with fury. "You son of a bitch, you lousy bastard, get your ass back out here..."

Her voice trailed.

She heard a sobbing sound, high pitched, almost like an animal wail in the night.

The light did not belong to her driver. Rather, it flooded over a macabre spectacle, that of a scarecrow...a scarecrow with a bizarre skeletal face stuffed with straw and with straw arms wrapped around a woman, a once flesh and blood woman, who dangled now from those straw arms. The thing's wire mouth dripped with blood.

So did the woman.

She lay, caught in that bizarre grip, white dress smeared with red, black hair falling around her, the way in which she was held reminding Ally of a ballet dancer in a bizarre pose.

The woman looked like...her!

Then Ally heard something, a dry cackling, rising into the air again like a sob that became a howl. The scarecrow started to laugh. It looked like the wire mouth moved.

Then Ally felt it. The first touch of the blade.

She screamed and screamed as she fell to the ground—her scream oddly echoing the scream she heard earlier, the scream that had taken the driver away, the scream she had thought to be part of a prank...

No prank.

Her pain was real. Her blood, spilling upon the ground...was real.

The dead...

It wasn't so safe among the dead after all...

As she watched the green/gray color of the night grow darker, she knew she was about to be...

Among them.

Chapter 1

"I'm still confused. I mean, it's nice—I mean, what's not to like? But why exactly are we here?" Michael Quinn asked Danni Cafferty, closing his eyes to luxuriate in the feel of the sun.

"Because Colleen is a friend of mine and she asked us to be here," Danni replied.

"But we didn't meet on a dating site," he reminded her. He glanced her way, a crooked smile on his lips. "As far as I know, as of yet, there are dating sites for those who want a cowboy or a farmer, dating sites for quick romances, those that figure out if you're financially and socially compatible. But no sites for those who lead slightly different lives dealing with slightly bizarre and often deadly situations," he pointed out.

Danni looked away sighing, and Quinn allowed himself a smile.

They had met after her father, an amazing old Scot, had died. After his death Danni discovered the "collectibles" her father kept in the basement—or destroyed at their shop on Royal Street in the French Quarter—had been cursed objects, creating havoc around them with often deadly results. She learned Angus Cafferty had been far more than just a nice guy— he'd been a really good man, quietly doing his best to help those in very peculiar trouble.

Quinn had been a cop, but he hadn't been anything good himself—other than a revered football hero. He had become too enamored of the lifestyle he'd been offered until he'd flatlined—had technically died in the ER—and been helped back to life by a mysterious presence.

Something, someone other than a doctor, had intervened. He'd known that—known he'd been offered a second chance. He'd seized upon it, and he'd changed his ways. Being offered a second chance at life, he'd become a good guy, confused at first, and then discovering evil did exist in ways most people never imagined. This was the beginning of the end of his police work.

Not that he hadn't been a good cop—he really had been, even if he liked to think of himself as decently humble. It just became far too difficult to explain at times what had happened at a bizarre incident—or to make others understand there was more to a situation than met the eye—or for that matter, more that met any form of rational thought.

So, Quinn left the police and got his private investigator's license. Some of his cases were humdrum—a way to keep up appearances. And an income. Others were so much more.

It was during this time he'd met Angus Cafferty, and after Angus's death...

Well, at first meeting, he'd thought Danni was a spoiled little princess. A beautiful princess with her deep auburn hair and brilliant blue eyes, but...

And Danni had thought him to be an incredible jerk. But working together, they'd discovered an attraction, and attraction had bloomed and become much more.

His days as a cop had been over by the time he'd met her. Quickly, she joined him in the work he'd once done with her father, and now Danni and he were always waist-deep in these jobs together.

Also, now he knew that he was a lucky, lucky man.

Not only did he have life itself, he had Danni.

He smiled at her now, taking a moment to bask in their situation, just lying here by the pool, popping in and out of the water when they chose. She was especially appealing in her swim attire, and always more so because she was oblivious to her own appearance. Watching her, he almost forgot he'd asked a question.

Until she answered him.

"Colleen has been incredibly successful with her dating site, so successful she's now created these resorts for people who have met through her site, or who want to meet others through the site but in the flesh, and for just any couples who wish to be here. It's a nice concept—a place for people. This is opening week for this property, and she's anxious, I believe, to see people are happy here. She believes we'll be the perfect happy couple for other happy couples to see or become! Also, being we are in Louisiana, she wants some of my artwork for the place, and she wants suggestions regarding other local artists. It's a great vacation, right? She also thinks we'll dress up, and therefore her other guests will dress up and make her Harvest Festival Ball great."

"It works for me," Quinn said. "I'm happy." He grinned and rolled over on his lounge chair, relaxing in the sun.

The sun was coming through the giant glass roof of the resort's indoor pool, but it still felt as if the real, unhindered rays were falling upon them.

They might be in the Deep South but fall could be chilly, and the concept of a heated pool in a controlled environment had been a good one for them.

He hated cold water. The pool in here was great. He knew he shouldn't question things at all—it was pretty darned amazing to be here. Both of them off from work. This was a true rarity.

Danni's shop, "The Cheshire Cat," would run fine with Billie McDougall watching over it. Billie had more experience with the shop than either of them really. Both managing the day-to-day running of their charming little boutique—and managing whatever strange object might arise causing havoc. A "Riff-Raff" lookalike from the "Rocky Horror Show", Billie had been with Angus Cafferty years before his death and had handled many a strange—or deadly—collectible in his day.

So, they were free to just be here at the Honeywell Lodge, Colleen Rankin's newest establishment for those who were looking for love—or had perhaps just fallen in love, like, or lust—were gathering.

It was a bit bizarre—watching the mating ritual in this venue had made him appreciate his relationship with Danni all the more. He'd now witnessed a lot of hesitant flirting, shy girls with no confidence, men who tripped over their words—and the confident and beautiful who just assumed they were going to be loved.

Still, it was a great resort. They were on vacation. There was a great stable and he hadn't been able to go riding in ages. They were now at the pool, he was feeling the sun. Well, they'd only had one night thus far, but their suite was beautiful; the whirlpool was big enough to allow for his height and size and another person—as in Danni, of course.

And still...

The sweet feel of luxury that had swept over him began to fade again—ridiculously.

He was restless. Maybe he didn't know how to relax. Not true. He knew down time was precious, they had embraced the lives that had fallen their way—but were still grateful to have found one another, and to steal free and special moments when they could. Things would happen—that made down time something to be enjoyed to the fullest. So why he couldn't just lie there, loving the feel of the sun, thinking about the trail ride—and other activities—they'd enjoy later, he didn't know.

So, go with it! He told himself. Even if he was going a little crazy, he needed to do it in silence. Let Danni have this special time.

She laughed suddenly, the sound soft and teasing, and very sexy.

Maybe he would forget his unease, yet.

"I tend to be the worrier," she reminded him. "You're the one always telling me there is no way to deal with what might be happening somewhere—that we live life!" she told him. She gave him a wonderful, ever-so-slightly wicked smile and settled back in her lounge chair as well. "We're on vacation!" she repeated. "We haven't had one in a while. Try to remember. Vacations are these nice events during which people don't work. They enjoy dining and dancing and lying around in the sun."

"Got it!" Quinn twisted again to look at her.

Not so hard to play this out, the shop, their home, and even Wolf—their incredible hybrid dog—were all in Billie's capable hands, and he had help. Bo Ray Tompkins was working at the shop, and down the street, should they need more help for any reason, they would find Natasha LaRouche, a voodoo priestess, a true practitioner in the religion. And should she have trouble, they could call on Father Ryan, and from there...

Vacation. He didn't need to worry; he needed to relax and enjoy this time with Danni. Enjoying time with her wasn't at all difficult. He was reminded of that every time he looked at her.

He arched a brow and attempted to give himself an exceptionally deep and sensual voice, "We're on vacation—where people are meeting people and getting romantic, right? Some come as couples. I mean, if I get this right, singles come to meet people they might have chatted with online already, right? But some have met, and they're in relationships. They're couples—and couples take the same room, and after a day at the pool, they may sink into their room's whirlpool tub, and then fool around on the satin sheets, huh?" He slid onto her lounge chair, "Of course, all the new people do all the things those newly in love—or lust—do to one another. Like the couples, they have a chance to spend the day at the pool, sink into a whirlpool in someone's room, and say the things people say. Like, 'your hair is as silken as the sheets. Your skin as soft...your eyes are the color of the sky on the clearest day, beautiful and crystal blue, and your hair is pure fire and when it brushes my flesh...'"

Danni looked around uneasily, frowning fiercely, and swatted him with the paper pool lunch menu she was holding. "Stop!"

"Hey—I was being romantic! That's what people do here, right?" he protested. "I was trying for romantic. Let's face it, I can promise you a lot of guys here are trying for sex—it's part of a romantic relationship, right—a true match? And we are in a relationship, deep, and sweet, and wonderful, and of course, hot, and..."

Danni arched a brow to him, grimacing, looking around at the others who were enjoying the indoor pool that day, some just chatting in lounge chairs, others laughing and hopping in and out of the pool.

He chuckled as he moved back to his lounge. He loved her with his whole heart; she was incredible, a sensual and passionate lover, and capable of both tremendous fun and seriousness when necessary. But she was a private person, and while they were at a romantic destination—with people showing displays of affection all around them—he knew she preferred demonstrative displays of affection to be saved for moments when they were alone. So did he.

He couldn't imagine his life without her now—even though, by the nature of their work, he spent far too much time worried about her. She was smart, street savvy, and so many other things. He knew he couldn't change her—anymore than she could change him.

That made their time here a surprise to him—but a damned nice one. A vacation. A true romantic getaway.

So why the hell can't I just sit back and enjoy it?

She laughed suddenly, leaning in a bit closer and lowering her head toward his. "Tease me in public, will you? Two can play at this. So...let's see...stretched out on the lounge, halfway turned toward me as you are, you look like the perfect poster boy for a 'young professional singles' dating site—ah, yes! Let's see...you're long, lean-muscled, and your bronze flesh is glistening from your last dip in the pool. Your rich, dark, damp hair is so sexy, haphazardly cast over your forehead."

She leaned even a bit closer, her eyes bright with mischief.

"Oh, yes, yum. You look like a cover model, boy," she told him.

"Hey!" he protested. "I was being perfectly honest. I love your hair and eyes and flesh...yeah, well, you know, silky bare flesh, and all."

She grinned. "And what I was saying was a compliment. You could be the model for Colleen's site!"

"You used the term 'boy,'" he said, shaking his head with a sigh. "Military, college, the academy, over ten years with the FBI—and you called me a boy!"

"All men are boys," she assured him.

He sighed, lying back. "Ah, such is romance! What do you think about pool-boy-man over there—tall, muscled, good-looking, about thirty or maybe thirty-plus—think I've seen him with a blond, a brunette, and a redhead so far at last night's mixer. He's covering all the bases."

"That's Albert Bennett—he's more or less a host this weekend. He works for Colleen in her security department, doing checks on people. It must be hard—her site is open to the public—but it is a dating site. She has to be careful she's not allowing kids, pedophiles, or what have you on. I guess Albert's position is computer security."

"Looks like he could be a poster boy. When did you meet him?"

"Jealous?" she teased.

"You know me better."

She nodded, still somewhat smiling. "I met him when I went to Colleen's offices on Canal Street the other day—after she called and asked us to come out this weekend. I also met Tracy Willard, Colleen's office manager. Perfect green-eyed redhead—I think she and Albert like each other, but they can't show it this weekend. Then again, she was chatting with others last night, too. Oh! And over there, on the far lounge—the kind-of-skinny-slightly-lost-looking fellow over there, the one wearing the trunks and rash-guard—that's Larry Blythe. He's involved with the business development. He helps Colleen make decisions about the site and now with her locations, and also about where and when she invests again. Colleen did something a bit different with each site—creating these places for people to meet—and he's her main man on that kind of thing."

Danni looked around. "I don't see her VP—Ally Caldwell—anywhere yet. Ally is also on the development team. That she's not here yet is kind of a surprise. Ally supported Colleen when she first wanted to expand her Internet site and was with her down in the trenches. Colleen wanted to supply a place for people to meet surrounded by others like them—or for those who had met, and wanted someplace...safe, I guess...to become couples. There are dozens of dating sites out there—but I think Colleen might have had the first business to open such places...fun and elegant havens where people could meet before committing to a relationship. Some sites tout paperwork that will make people compatible, and some exist just for people who pass by one another to start off with a quickie or one-night stand. Colleen believes in seeing, deciding, getting to meet in person, face-to-face."

"It's the modern world. You can go online and find just about anything, why not love?" He asked lightly.

"She doesn't believe paperwork can make you compatible—even if you both have the same interests. If you don't have chemistry, well, it will just never be a real romance."

"Sometimes, though, it is good when you share a few interests," he said.

"Hm. Well, thankfully, most people don't have to share one of our—interests!" Danni said.

"Hey, your dad's 'collecting' did bring us together!" he said. "Anyways, I'm very happy to be here—thrilled to be a guest—and the price couldn't be better!"

"Especially since the price is free!"

He frowned, looking toward the garden area beyond the pool.

"So, all these people are looking for love...or something?"

Danni laughed. "Something like that. Anyway, the big party is planned for Martinmas. It's really a French holiday in honor of St. Martin, born in Hungary, but one of the saints who did much for France. Ally pushed to open now because they really get into the whole concept of celebrating harvest time. The concept travelled over Europe and was carried here along with many of the French settlers and the Acadians. It also became something of a harvest festival, and they celebrate the harvest here along with his saint's day. It's a big deal. But like all things once religious, it's also a big party. I guess in the old days it had a lot to do with praying for or being thankful for a rich harvest—so people could survive through the winter."

"That makes it a great day for people at a dating service...meeting site? Ah, wait, never mind—I guess a good harvest could mean many things!"

She gave him a slight punch on the arm. "Behave."

"Why?" he queried lightly. "I mean...this is all about love, right? Or affairs, or..."

Danni did indeed wear her bikini exceptionally well, creating a teasing situation that had already begun to make him contemplate the trip back up to their suite. Maybe they'd head up soon, Quinn thought. That would keep his mind off the strange worry tugging at him. Plenty of privacy there. And never spoke the words.

He opened his mouth to suggest that very thing, but as he looked at Danni he could see past her toward the archways leading from the indoor pool into the bordering patio, and from there back into the sumptuous lobby. Before he could form the words, he saw a disturbing sight. Something seemed to slam against him as if in answer to the restless foreboding that had been tugging at his mind.

"Your friend, our hostess, Colleen is coming," he sat up, his body filling with tension, a frown knitting his brow, "with people I know," he added, his tone growing darkly curious.

His senses had been keen. This was it, then, whatever it was he'd felt was coming, and the playful peace they'd been enjoying was abruptly at an end.

Colleen was looking for them specifically, Quinn knew, as she entered the indoor pool area along with two men, one of whom he recognized—and who shouldn't have been here.

"That's Jake Larue with her" he said.

When Quinn had been a detective with the NOLA force, Larue had been his partner, and he'd been on hand for many an incident since.

"What the hell is he doing out here?" he muttered.

Danni quickly followed his gaze. "What?" she murmured. "Larue? I hope nothing is wrong at home. I mean, he's with NOLA. Why would he be out here?"

"I'm sure nothing is wrong at home. Billie would have called. Whatever it is, we're about to find out. You friend is headed straight to us with Larue in tow, and it looks like another cop. I'm willing to bet he's with the parish police. I just might know him, too. We were out this way just about a year or so ago."

Colleen Rankin was a tiny woman with brown curls, warm brown eyes to match and usually a bubbly personality that was friendly and kind and contagious. There was nothing cheerful or bubbly about her now. She looked more than serious as she drew closer; she appeared to have been crying.

She walked just ahead of Larue and the other man. Larue, of course, was in plain clothes. He was wearing a work-day gray-suit and tailored shirt—with a slight bulge beneath his jacket that indicated he was wearing a holster and service arm. He was an even six feet, close-cropped brown hair, level eyes, and had an all-around appearance of competence and determination.

The second man was older with dark hair showing white at the edge and steely gray eyes in a well-lined face.

Yep, parish police! Quinn thought.

"Larue—and another cop," Danni murmured, her glance at Quinn assuring him she was now dreading what was coming, too.

Something bad.

They both knew it.

"Parish Police—plainclothes homicide," Quinn said. He got a better look at the second man coming toward them and memory kicked in. He had worked with him not just recently, but also several years back on a drug-smuggling case that had left bodies in New Orleans and half of the state.

"Damn," he murmured. "It's Peter Ellsworth. I've worked with him before. I'm pretty sure this means there is a body somewhere."

Quinn quickly stood, and Danni did likewise, ready to meet Colleen and the detectives.

Colleen was distraught, and though she had definitely been crying, she was now somewhat composed—until she neared Danni, and then she rushed forward, throwing herself into Danni's arms.

Danni instinctively wrapped her arms around her friend, looking at Quinn over Colleen's head, her eyes filled with care and confusion.

Quinn had recently met Colleen Rankin, their hostess for the weekend, after Danni had come to tell him about the opening of the resort—and how they had been invited. He knew she and Danni had gone to school together, though they hadn't seen each other in ages because Colleen's main base had been New York City. Colleen was friendly, open, sincere, and enthusiastic—and easy to like. Danni had told him Colleen was one of the most honestly nice and caring individuals she had ever met—which made it almost surprising Colleen had not just done well but flourished in the business of creating an online dating service—she liked and trusted people so much, she might have been easily taken.

However, she had been smart enough to bring more skeptical help into her business.

She was usually accompanied by one of her VPs—trusted employees who kept her from giving away the entire barn during negotiations on a deal.

Today she was alone—except for Detectives Larue and Peter Ellsworth.

Larue nodded gravely at Quinn and Danni.

"Quinn," Ellsworth said, offering his hand to Quinn and nodding to Danni as Colleen remained crushed against her like a child.

Danni was almost five-ten. She offered an encompassing hold, and while she was slim enough herself, Colleen appeared extremely tiny and fragile in her arms.

Colleen was babbling as she clung to Danni.

"Composure...composure...I have guests. This is my grand opening weekend. Oh, my God! One of my guests went into the cemetery; and it's so horrible, so, so horrible. No, no, what am I saying? My employee, a right-hand man...woman...I mean. Of course, it has nothing to do with the resort, except it's my Ally! I couldn't understand why she was late...why she wasn't answering her phone. I tried calling back to the office...a car picked her up, just as she planned, but it's gone and she's..."

Colleen broke off with a sob.

"Dead," Peter Ellsworth offered. He looked at Colleen with a cross between compassion and hard-worn patience and then turned back to Quinn. "Larue told me you were here, Quinn, and you tend to be excellent at...this kind of thing." He took a long look at Danni.

He'd met her, at least briefly, Quinn thought, and he had to know she worked with him on his investigations.

"Sorry, Quinn," Larue said.

"On vacation, I understand," Ellsworth told him apologetically and added, "but with your home being in New Orleans, and now this..."

This what? He wanted to shout.

"It's all right. What happened?" he managed to ask calmly.

Neither Ellsworth nor Larue had a chance to answer.

"Ally. Ally is dead. She was on her way here," Colleen said, trying to speak clearly. "One of our couples went back to see the cemetery...it's rather famous. They found her, and the others, and...oh, God."

"We were hoping you would be good enough to return to the scene with us; the medical examiner is on his way as well," Peter Ellsworth said to Quinn. "The scene is—quite bizarre."

"Of course," Quinn said, looking at Larue, his frown questioning his friend's appearance here.

"It mimics a death scene found in a small family cemetery in Uptown, NOLA," Larue said.

"When?"

"We found the victims...last night. Victims...well, two were victims, the other was already dead," Larue said. "Yeah, yeah, I realize how confusing this is as I try to explain—we need to get to the crime scene, you'll understand better there."

"I do hope you have some kind of a touch of magic. This is going to get the whole state into an uproar...two in two days," Ellsworth said.

Yes—they were confusing him.

"You'll come, now? Right away?" Ellsworth asked.

"Of course," Quinn assured him. He liked the man. He was a Parish officer who knew not just his base—Iberia Parish—but all of Quinn's beloved Louisiana. He worked well with others and was an interesting man who excelled at listening, which made him invaluable when facts needed to be gathered and put together like puzzle pieces.

He just hoped Larue would make sure he didn't demand explanations for all of their findings.

"We need five minutes," Quinn told the detectives. "Clothing," he added with a grimace.

"We?" Peter Ellsworth asked, frowning, and then studying Danni again. "It's not—pleasant. And," he paused, uncomfortable as he spoke, "we're trying to keep the general populace away."

"Danni isn't the general populace," Quinn said.

"Quinn and I have worked together many times," Danni informed him. "I'm something of an expert on...bizarre rituals and strange behavior," she added. "My father was a collector; we did a great deal of research on many...unusual objects."

"How, uh...well, fitting, I guess," Detective Ellsworth said, looking at Quinn.

"Sir, we did meet briefly—and you know I'm involved with Quinn's cases," Danni said firmly. "I really provide insight and...research."

Quinn lowered his eyes; there was no other way to explain Danni's relationship with law enforcement.

Let Ellsworth wonder. He knew he wasn't leaving without Danni.

She was an odd combination of dignity and sensuality as they stood there—a lovely form in her bathing suit, tall and straight and professional as well. Perhaps it was her face, features composed and confident, heedless of the opinions of others, aware of her own abilities.

Either that, or she just didn't want Quinn leaving alone. Especially when the matter had to do with her friend.

"It's...a bizarre and ugly scene," Ellsworth told her. "Perhaps..."

"I'll be fine," Danni added, "murder is never pleasant. It's always ugly."

Chapter 2

The cemetery was something right out of a Hollywood set. Even by day, it seemed to be shrouded in a gray mist. They'd entered through creaking filigreed iron gates created beneath an artistic arch. They'd passed by old stones and newer stones, slanted in the ground by age. Above ground tombs and vaults and small mausoleums, the typical type found in the "cities of the dead" that were part of the culture and architecture that made New Orleans known for its treatment of the dead, were found here also.

They reached the murder site through long, winding, overgrown trails.

Detective Ellsworth had been right.

Bizarre was barely adequate for what they came upon. Ugly was sadly accurate.

Danni had seen the bizarre and the ugly before—and of course, the tragic and the sad. However, when they arrived at the crime scene, the site of the corpses was nothing less than bone-chilling. Even as the word came to mind, she silently chastised herself—no pun intended.

It was something straight out of the most gruesome slasher movie. Bones littered the ground. There were three corpses; each had been set up on a crossed pole in a manner to mimic a scarecrow. The corpses had straw sticking from their sleeves, necklines, and shoes.

The medical examiner had arrived; he was busy on a foldable ladder, inspecting the corpse to the far right.

Danni certainly didn't have a medical degree, but it appeared from first glance at least one of the victims—Ally Caldwell—had died from a vicious knife attack. Her body and the straw stuffed around her were marked with red stains that must certainly be blood.

Great quantities of it.

"Cursed Yvette," Peter Ellsworth muttered beneath his breath as they approached.

Danni glanced at him quickly. Cursed Yvette? Different. Every kid had heard of "Bloody Mary" and seen some kind of movie or show in which, if you said the name three times, good old Bloody Mary hopped out to create mayhem and murder.

There had definitely been some mean mayhem and murder here.

But "Cursed Yvette?" That was a new one to her, but she assumed, there had to be a legend here that was much the same.

The victims, other than Ally, had been displayed in a like manner, though she wasn't sure how they had met their end. It was hard to judge what their appearance in life might have been. They were covered in straw, cemetery dirt, and what appeared to be a wealth of moss that hung from many of the great oaks in the area.

The first corpse was that of an old man. Thin, heavily wrinkled, and possessing a headful of gray hair and a gray beard. She saw he, too, was covered in red—his beard was covered and sticky with crimson. His face had been all but cut away, leaving little flesh and bold areas of exposed bone.

The second corpse was Ally Caldwell. She had been perhaps in her mid-thirties. Her hair had been dark, almost black, and appeared stygian. She was missing her shoes, but they were down with the bones—bright red stilettos that seemed bizarre next to blood and bone.

The third body set up on a pole—arms stretched out—was that of a younger man, dressed in a business suit. His hair had been dark as well. It was difficult to discern anything more about him.

"This took time," Quinn said, standing very still as he surveyed the scene, his eyes sharp as he kept his distance, staring at the corpses. He turned, looking back to the old arched, iron gate. Outside, the police had set up a cordon—not that it seemed there was anyone out there to cordon out. They were deep enough into the cemetery that someone driving by wouldn't see the area of the corpses.

The killer knew the cemetery and knew it was mostly left as what it was—old and all but abandoned—other than being a mecca for the rare tourist who made it to this area.

"Yes, it took time," Detective Ellsworth agreed. "This isn't a place easily seen from the street like the big cemeteries in Metairie. Maybe it should be, but it's not a tourist haunt. Until Colleen Rankin opened her resort, there just wasn't enough up here to attract anyone but a die-hard would-be ghost hunter, or sometimes, a real hunter. Lots of deer, that's for sure."

"But we're not that far from Lafayette, New Iberia, and other cities and towns with at least fair-sized populations."

"The woman is...Ally Caldwell?" Quinn asked, looking at Danni.

Danni nodded.

"Two of the guests from Miss Rankin's opening, love old cemeteries, and they were down here fooling around. They hysterically called 911." Ellsworth hesitated. "Have to admit, we thought it might be a scary display a few of the local teens had set up—you can buy all kinds of creepy stuff these days that look like the real thing. We are looking at Martinmas and the harvest festival events that go on. There's always locals who think a little spooking at this time is appropriate. Officer Finn McKinney responded when the call came, and...well, here we are. Bizarre. I don't know if this is looking like cult or ritual or— I don't know what. But Miss Rankin said you were here, Quinn, when she called the parish." He paused. "We don't know who the other two victims are—we're waiting for the medical examiner to finish with his preliminaries. We'll try fingerprints...dental records. And well, hell, this really smacks of something frightening; and with you being here, and Larue looking to solve his own murder and that being back in New Orleans where he'd have brought you in as a consultant...well, here, you could see it all at the onset." He looked at Danni again. "Hope that's all right. And, uh, that you're involved, too."

"Fine. Glad you brought me in," she answered. "Crime scene techs have been over the ground?"

There were two workers wearing yellow parkas with "Crime Scene Unit" printed on them. Both were looking over an area in front of Ally Caldwell's body.

"They've started—take the marked path, if you will," Ellsworth said.

Danni followed Quinn as they carefully stepped to the cone-marked path that had already been swept by the crime scene investigators.

They would have picked up any scrap of paper, cigarette butt, bottle, can, or anything else at all that had been cast off or pushed aside—including the straw that still littered the area.

Straw—for scarecrows.

The medical examiner—a man of about fifty with white-blond hair and a serious, competent look—looked back at them from the ladder as he surveyed the bodies.

"No one has touched these bodies before I got here, right?" he asked, frowning.

"No, sir," Ellsworth said, and the others nodded.

The medical examiner climbed down—and then back up between the last two "scarecrow" victims. He took a few minutes and stepped down.

He walked the few feet to where they were standing. "This is...well, I need to do the autopsies. But I'm going to go out on a limb and saying cause of death was exsanguination, and method was a very sharp knife or blade of some kind."

"They were killed last night?" Quinn asked, not offering to shake the M.E.'s gloved hand.

The man shrugged. "Two of them, anyway. Sometime after midnight. Except...sorry, who are you?"

"Sorry," Ellsworth muttered. "Danni, Quinn, this is Dr. Glenn Harper, best man in the parish," he said. "Michael Quinn and..."

"Danielle Cafferty," Larue said. He paused just a second and added. "She's an expert." He didn't say exactly what it was she was an expert in.

Harper nodded and looked curiously at Danni as well. "The Cheshire Cat?" he asked her.

"Yes," she said. "My dad started the shop. You've been there?"

He nodded. "I knew your father," he said simply. "Good to see you here; you could possibly shed some light on a mind that could come up with something so brutal and..."

"Also, preplanned," she said.

"Have you ever come up against anything like this?" he asked.

"Like this...no," Danni said.

"Dr. Harper, you said *two of them* after midnight. And then you added the word *except*. What is the *except?*" Quinn asked.

"Except for the first corpse," Harper said. "That man has been dead at least a week; he has been embalmed—and interred or buried somewhere, I would assume. And then...well, dug up or dug out. And turned into a scarecrow."

"But there's blood all over him. And his face is gone," Danni said.

"The blood is borrowed, and if you look close, you'll see it was easy enough for the killer to hack away flesh and get down to bone. There are three bodies, but two murders here. As to the third body, I have no idea. As soon as I do know something, you'll know it. I'll be starting on the bodies first thing tomorrow."

"May I take a closer look at them now?" Quinn asked him.

"Of course. My assistants will step back when you need; the photographer will be taking more pictures," the M.E. said. "Mr. Quinn, your reputation precedes you."

Quinn turned to look at Danni, a guarded look of query and surprise on his face. She shrugged, indicating Larue was walking right behind them, heading toward the bizarre display of the dead.

She watched as the morgue assistants stepped back, letting Quinn come close to the bodies; he didn't touch them, lest he contaminate any evidence that was found.

One by one, he began to slowly inspect them.

As he did so, Danni found she had to turn away.

Their strange—and under the radar work and perhaps their lives in general—had brought her to many an old cemetery and graveyard.

Because of it, she had also had a chance to witness the dead, the remains of the human shell, sometimes still in a semblance of life, sometimes with that human shell torn to ribbons.

This strange, abandoned cemetery seemed exceptionally odd all on its own. There was no old church—in the past, burial grounds and graveyards surrounded churches. In general, people had started to discover that burying the dead near the living could cause illness; and thus cemeteries, or burial grounds, began to be moved out beyond the lines of a city. But in the Christian world, the dead were to be buried in consecrated ground; and it was customarily in the late 1700s or early 1800s that the separate and individual cemetery—privately or municipally run—found popularity. In Victorian days, the concept of a cemetery being as pretty as a picnic ground, a good place to come to honor the dead, gained hold, and many such cemeteries were filled with exquisite tombs and statuary and benches where the visitor could long sit and remember those lost.

This was...

An abandoned mishmash. A quick glance showed her most of the old stones could no longer be read—no esteemed historians had been here to re-etch words of commemoration. There were numerous statues in many sections. Behind her and to her right, there was group of brick mausoleums, all of them looking like little hills, since time had sunk them deeper into the earth and nature had covered them with grass and weeds. Here and there, crosses rose high above an in-ground grave or a tomb, and there were the customary lambs here and there—indicative of children's graves—along with saints, obelisks and more.

Detective Ellsworth was standing by Danni and apparently noted the way she was looking around. "Thirty acres," he told her. "Started off hundreds of years ago with the first wave of French immigration. Back in those days, the French were settling southern Louisiana even before you had the 'L'Acadians' coming down from Canada. I don't think there are many surviving tombstones from then. Though over there—those brick vaults that go into the ground—those are very old tombs started up by some of the first settlers to this area." He gave her a semi-smile. "I happen to know this because my mother's family goes way back here from the French. Those vaults were originally for immediate families. If you lost children at a young age, they would fit just fine. Usually room in those vaults for four or five large coffins and a little altar. At one time, people went into the vaults and visited their dead and prayed at the altars. Most are probably trashed by now. Grave robbers and vandals have been around since recorded history."

"Yes, I've seen similar vaults before," Danni said.

"But you've never been out here?"

She shook her head. "I've spent time in Broussard, New Iberia, Lafayette...but I've never been here before."

"So, what do you make of this? You know, a killer could have stuck a few bodies into one of those old vaults—they're all falling apart, and I'm willing to bet the corpses have long been with nothing but bone-dust and bits and pieces of whatever metal they were buried with. Here, the murders could have been easily hidden. This guy..."

"Display was important," Danni said.

"Yeah, so he cut up a man and woman—and then dug up a corpse to go with them. There's no I.D. on the man yet, but half of his face is gone. And as you know, we only have Miss Caldwell's identity because the couple who wanted to explore the cemetery found the bodies and sent pictures right away—

thankfully, to the cops and not so thankfully to Miss Rankin as well. Glad she wasn't out here—she might have been trying to pull the corpse of her friend down to resuscitate." He paused, nodding to the corpses. "But had you met this woman at all, this Allison Caldwell?"

"I saw her briefly when I met Colleen at her offices," Danni said. "I didn't really know her, I only knew about her."

"Was she into any kind of...?"

"Any kind of?" Danni asked.

"Witchcraft, rituals, rites, vampirism—anything like that?"

Danni hiked her brows in surprise. "I don't know anything about her personally. I do know she's been an assistant to Colleen for a long time. She's a vice president of the company. Sorry, she was a vice president of the company. Colleen loved her and she, along with a few of her other top employees formed her inner circle, because Colleen is a people person herself—not much of a business woman. From what I understand, Ally was an incredible whiz at business."

"Seems like Colleen's done well," Ellsworth noted.

"Yes, she's done well, but she always wanted people around to keep her in check—to see she didn't give everything away. Colleen started her site because she had minor criticisms of most of the other sites out there. She especially felt it didn't matter what it said on paper—you were only compatible if you met and all the right chemistry was there."

Ellsworth turned to look at her. "So, the dead woman—her assistant. Allison Caldwell. Most of the daters or 'Meet Me' people wouldn't have known her. Only other employees."

"The new lodge welcomed its first guests yesterday at a mixer. Colleen had it set so people could come in a day or two before her Harvest Festival ball. Ally was so much more than an assistant. A VP. She was held up at the NOLA office and left New Orleans late. A car service came for her, and she should have arrived last night," Danni said. "That's my understanding."

Ellsworth stared at Quinn as he investigated the bodies—the three aligned, like human scarecrows, complete with straw.

"What kind of a mind does this?" he asked.

"Someone apparently making a statement," Danni said. "As I said," she added softly, "someone created a display to make that statement."

He turned back to her. "What would that statement be?" he asked. "How the hell—and why?—would anyone create such a statement in a small NOLA cemetery and then here?"

She forced a smile. "I'm sorry, Detective Ellsworth, I just don't know. The number three seems to have meant something—either that, or the image perhaps being religious—Christ on the cross, flanked by thieves. The killer committed two murders—according to the M.E. Gruesome murders, with a knife. I'm thinking male because biologically, males tended to be stronger and better at wielding a knife quickly and efficiently. That doesn't, however, exclude a woman. Two murders were committed—one body was dug up. I didn't know interments or burials still took place here, but—"

"They don't," Ellsworth said flatly. "The parishes and the state have been arguing over this place for at least a decade. It's been so out of the way until now that no one really cared. The nearest town, Perryville, is so small it barely had a name. Except Colleen Rankin has now put it on the map. Still, if you've been around, you've seen. It's really one main street with a bank, a few restaurants, grocery store, doctor's office—a few other businesses, including a major retailer of heavy hardware and tools for local farmers and ranchers. The cemetery straddles two parishes, making it hard for anyone to get it all together and do anything. This..."

His voice trailed. He looked at Danni, as if waiting for her to speak.

"You are here because you research this kind of thing, right? You've seen the bizarre over the years, because of your father's collecting?"

She shrugged, took a breath and decided he really wanted an answer from her—and it would mean something to him.

"I'm going to suggest this scene resembles the work of a narcissist. It's a tableau that says, 'you will see me.' The killer appears to have been organized—this took time and thought especially since there are two crime scenes—here and New Orleans. The straw came in from somewhere else—just as the man who was already dead was brought in from somewhere else. The medical examiner said the old man had been embalmed—so that would suggest he was buried or interred somewhere near. I imagine they will discover his identity fairly quickly."

"Well," he said at last. "I'm sorry for your friend. All her plans for a grand, romantic opening, and she winds up with a dead employee. In addition to whoever the murdered man is—

and whoever the already-dead guy might be. Anyway, so much for romance. Cops of all kinds will be prowling around everywhere—and mostly at the resort."

"You're going to have to do whatever is necessary," Danni said. "Excuse me. I'm going to take a bit of a walk around—out of the crime scene, of course."

She smiled weakly at him and turned, fascinated by the brick mounds that were so covered with grass and bracken that they might have been tiny hills.

Old. Very old. Nature had all but reclaimed them. There were three; she walked around them once and then again.

It was on the second return that she saw the small opening at the base of the first, as if it were a small crevice into a cave.

She glanced back to where the medical examiner and his assistants were now taking down the corpses, and Quinn was in conversation with both Larue and Detective Ellsworth. They were a bit of a distance away.

She knew she should get one of them before exploring, but their conversation appeared to be intense, and Ellsworth seemed very curious regarding her opinions—when she really shouldn't have been giving any.

And she wanted to see more.

Having spent so much time with Quinn, she never went anywhere without a small but powerful flashlight; she was also armed with a bottle of pepper spray she could draw from her bag with a speed that might well rival the draw of many a seasoned agent. She just wanted to peek in.

Danni waved her light at the hole then hunkered down to look in. By moving the light around, she could get a good look at the space within. Whatever burials had taken place here, there were not as many bodies as there might have been at one time. There were several tombs in the room, but they didn't hold bodies, only bones, crushed by time and the elements. The slabs which had lain over the tombs had been shoved aside, their seals broken, each in various stages of crumbled dust and broken chunks.

Danni frowned curiously—she couldn't see if anything remained in the tombs down deep.

Her mind was racing.

Why dislodge the dead?

Some, at least, had been rudely disinterred. Bones, bone fragments, and skulls lay about the walls of the vault, haphazardly tossed about, eerie in the pinpoint light, caught in strange shadows by way of the focused light.

Then, of course, the more pressing question.

Did this vandalism of an old and abandoned tomb have anything to do with the horrific display of victims upon poles, created to resemble a macabre tableau of bloodied scarecrows?

The cemetery was crawling with police and crime scene personal. That should make it fine for her to crawl into a hole—within easy screaming distance of all the law-enforcement. She hesitated just a minute—she could get someone to come in with her. But they were all busy, deep in conversation, theory, and argument. She was close enough to help should she need it, and so she crawled through the tomb opening, carefully aiming her light about as she did so.

The tombs or vaults had not been created as anything grand like the great pyramids of Egypt, no long shafts of any kind—and it was a short distance to the ground from the opening hole.

Running her light over the inside of the vault—half beneath the ground and half above it—she saw it contained five concrete tombs. Each designed originally, she assumed, to hold one body, or possibly, two, maybe even three.

She heard a noise and a skittering sound, causing her to jump. Training her light around, she saw one small rat scurrying into a pile of dead leaves and dust. She'd make sure any rat in the tomb knew she was coming. She wasn't terrified of the little creatures, but she didn't really want to be bitten either.

Walking over to the first tomb, she trained her light into it. There were no bones, no earthly remains of the original occupant.

Instead, there was straw.

The same straw used to create the "scarecrows" of the dead displayed in the cemetery?

Moving from tomb to tomb, looking within the first three, she found more and more.

More and more...straw.

Puzzled, she restrained from moving the straw; it was time to get Quinn and those working the crime scene.

She was tempted to pick up a bone to shift the straw around but decided there had been enough disrespect done to the dead here—while others would surely examine the bones here in time, she didn't want to disturb the tomb in any way.

Had this been long in the planning? Or had something been going on here long before they had heard about the murder of Allison Caldwell?

Had they found straw at the murder scene in NOLA?

She started to head over to the fourth tomb, certain all would be the same.

But that time, as she shifted her light, a shadow seemed to loom high against the far wall of the vault. Shadows were natural with her small light in the darkness of the tomb, but there was a sixth sense inside her shouting that the shadow had been too big, it hadn't fallen into the realm of what should have naturally occurred.

Time to get out.

It was possible a killer lurked here. That he had waited, eager to watch the result of his handiwork.

She backed carefully in the direction of the hole in the earth by which she had entered. When she reached the hard earth and stone wall, she paused and turned, ready to crawl back out.

But she froze.

There was darkness covering the entry, as if the sun had fallen, or...

As if someone had come to cover it over, to prevent her from ever leaving this realm of the dead.

Chapter 3

"We usually get the bodies checked in on one day, and start the autopsies on the next," Dr. Harper said, removing his gloves as he joined Quinn, Larue, and Peter Ellsworth where they stood, about five feet back from the staked "scarecrows" that held the three bodies, "but, in this case, I'm going to get started as soon as I can get them back, photographed, and cleaned up."

Two assistants had come along with the M.E., and they were busy working with two of the crime scene techs to get the bodies down and into ambulances to convey them to the parish morgue.

"Thank you," Peter Ellsworth told him. "Expediency in this might be everything."

"You think it has something to do with old harvest fest sacrifices, or voodoo—or some other weird cult?" Dr. Harper asked.

"Nothing to do with the real religion of voodoo," Quinn said. Dr. Harper looked at him, frowning.

"I, uh, didn't mean to offend," Harper said, frowning.

"Sorry," Quinn said. "We have a friend who is a voodoo priestess in New Orleans. Trust me, murder has nothing to do with anyone who adheres to voodoo as their belief—human sacrifices are the stuff of movie fare or a sick cult—as with any other form of religion. If you are a true believer, you don't do harm to others—it would come back at you several times over." He shrugged. "One of my friend's best friends is another best friend of ours, and he's a Catholic priest. I hear about theology all the time."

"Know them all," Larue said. "Good people. But that doesn't mean some whacked out person doesn't use voodoo—or even Christianity—in some bizarre way."

"That's true—anyone can twist anything just about any way they want," Quinn agreed. "But nothing I'm seeing here is reflective of voodoo."

"No," Larue said quietly. "This is some kind of...old autumn ritual we know nothing about?" he asked. "A sick twist on...I don't know what."

One of the crime scene investigators was searching the ground close to where they stood. She had apparently overheard and was looking at them as if she wished to speak, but perhaps worried that it wasn't her place to do so. She was a young woman in her early twenties with dark hair pulled back, large brown eyes, and a wide, friendly face. Her appearance was so young, fresh, and sweet, it seemed odd she was wearing a parish parka and working at such a bloody crime scene.

"Hey!" Quinn said to her. "Do you know anything about the people around here or this place in particular?"

"Legends." she said softly.

Peter Ellsworth let out a long sigh. "Cursed Yvette, right?" He looked from Jake Larue to Quinn. "Local legend—a Cajun girl fell in love with a rich Englishman. His mother killed her, and in turn, a year later the mother was murdered. Kind of like our version of 'Bloody Mary.' You're not supposed to say Yvette's name in the cemetery or something like that."

"No, nothing to do with Yvette," the young woman said. "I'm Mandy, by the way, CSI Mandy Haverhill."

"This is Detective Jake Larue out of New Orleans," Quinn said, indicating Jake by way of an introduction. "And with the Parish, Detective Peter Ellsworth—"

"Mandy and I know each other, of course," Ellsworth said, nodding toward her.

Mandy nodded and looked at Quinn. "And you're Detective—?"

"Nope. I'm Quinn. Just Quinn. Private Investigator out of New Orleans, so I'm happy to hear more about local legends."

"Really?" Mandy asked, hesitant.

"Incredibly interested," Quinn said, indicating the scarecrow poles. "Someone has been delving into some kind of legend, so it appears."

Mandy nodded gravely.

"Okay," she said. "Yes, there's the story about Yvette, and it has gone on for...well, hundreds of years, I suppose. She was supposedly Cajun, and then the English or Americans or English Americans were moving out here, and at the time, they really didn't mix. Enraged, the boy's mother supposedly killed Yvette, only to be mysteriously killed herself in the same spot a year or so later. People love to use stories like that and embellish them. Every several decades or so, a mean person is supposedly murdered out here—Yvette's spirit or ghost helping rid the world of those who would ruin other lives."

"Was Ally supposed to be a nasty person?" Larue asked Quinn.

Quinn shrugged. "I have no idea. I imagine that just about anyone in the world might be considered to be a mean or nasty person by someone else. But," he said, turning back to the young crime scene worker, "you seem to know about another legend? What is it?"

She hesitated, glancing to the poles that had held the "scarecrows."

"So local legend," Quinn murmured, glancing at Larue.

How the hell had it started in NOLA then?

"It revolves around the number three—superstitions, I guess. But the very first burial here was that of three people. Supposedly, the priest spoke about the number three that day—birth, life, and death. The circle of life. And more. Supposedly, bad things happen in threes."

She stopped speaking, looking at them all. They weren't responding.

"Well, the legend goes that soon after the cemetery was begun—even before Perryville, the nearest little town was established—we had a night in which three bizarre murders took place. It was right around Martinmas—of course, though, you know how legends go. It might have been January, if what happened really happened at all. One woman and two men were hideously hacked to pieces—and left in the cemetery on stakes." Her voice dropped to a whisper. "Sometimes, when you hear the story, it's said the woman had been a witch, and she had killed her husband and their handyman, and then been murdered herself by a friend who came upon the scene. Not wanting to be blamed for the murders, he'd set them up as he thought the witches might set them up—on poles, or as it being the harvest time, as..."

"Scarecrows?" Quinn asked. "To do with...protecting the crops, or the harvest, or."

She nodded solemnly. "Then the other version is the woman had something in her possession that could cause people to go insane—and kill others or themselves. Again, the same friend—I guess—came along and turned the tables on her. How he had the charm or talisman or whatever on him and didn't kill himself, I don't know, but the story goes two ways after that, too. One, that the talisman was buried with them. Another version has it that someone has the talisman in their home, though I don't know how many homes were around at that time. But that it's believed that it is still out there—somewhere."

"Well," Larue said skeptically, "it wouldn't be easy to kill others, kill yourself—and bind yourself up on a pole like a scarecrow. But the number three..."

"And the versions all have scarecrows," Ellsworth said.

"It doesn't matter what the legend was, true or not true in any version, if someone is playing on it, we have to find them," Quinn said flatly. "The legend says something causes you to go insane and kill others—and maybe yourself. Maybe not. Maybe the kind farmer was the one who went insane and killed everyone. Somehow, he gained control and got rid of the talisman—before it got to him."

"Or he invented the story to get away with murder," Ellsworth said.

"The number three," Larue said thoughtfully. "Well, we have three. Maybe that means we have to catch a killer, but he's done with his killing spree."

"New Orleans—and then Perryville. I think we have to catch a killer before there are three more," Quinn said, watching as the last of the corpses was lowered from a pole and onto a gurney with a body bag.

Legends were stories, of course. Enlarged, exaggerated, twisted, and turned.

But they often had a base in fact.

He was already wondering what kind of talisman might exist in the environs of Mount Misery and the cemetery.

***

The shadow had moved; everything was as it had been. Still Danni waited, watching for a few minutes before she crawled back out of the tomb.

As she did so, she heard a sharp, startled cry.

"Oh, my God!"

There was a couple that had apparently been leaning back against the other side of the little hillock that had formed over the in-ground tombs. They had used the natural slant to lean against as they talked...or...whatever.

As she exited the tomb, they must have thought she was the dead rising. The woman jumped to her feet; the man who had been at her side did the same. Then again, she was just as stunned to see them. She had thought the cemetery had been closed off—the medical examiner's van was at the gates along with several vehicles belonging to the parish investigators.

After a minute, Danni realized she knew them both—or had, at least, met them at the lodge mixer party last night. She was Tracy Willard, a pretty, vivacious redhead, Colleen's office manager from her base of operation in New York City. He was Trent Anderson, a local scion, so Danni had heard, land owner, investor, local millionaire—very, very eligible —and all-around supreme catch for many a young single woman with high hopes for a wealthy match-up.

"Danni!" Tracy said, her voice breathy. She was still shaking, Danni thought.

"Miss Cafferty," Trent murmured, obviously still surprised, though certainly no longer frightened. "Um—what are you doing, crawling around in tombs?"

She stared at them both. "How did you get in here? There's a crime scene less than a football field away."

"What?" they asked in unison.

Danni shook her head. "You didn't hear? There were murders committed here last night. A member of the Rankin group who was on her way out here and a man—as yet unknown. How on earth did you get in here without passing the authorities?"

"Murder." Tracy said. "One of Colleen's people?" she said, her voice barely a whisper.

"I'm so sorry," Danni murmured. Of course. Tracy knew Ally Caldwell; they were both from Colleen's New York base.

"What the hell?" Trent said, walking around Danni to look toward the front half of the cemetery—and the personnel still working the site.

"Oh, my God!" he whispered, hurrying back.

"Who? Who? Oh..." Tracy said.

"I'm so sorry," Danni said quickly. *Not a good way to find out a friend and co-worker had died.*

"Who?" Tracy whispered again. She looked as if she was going to fall, but Trent Anderson was immediately back at her side, supporting her.

Danni wasn't sure she had ever felt more awkward.

She took a deep breath. "I'm so sorry," she said again—before taking another deep breath. She had to just say it; if Tracy had been at the lodge, she'd have known by now.

"Ally. Um, Allison Caldwell."

"Ally," Tracy said, eyes wide as she stared at her.

Danni nodded.

Tracy closed her eyes and took a deep breath. "Ally," she murmured.

The woman didn't burst into tears, nor did she waver. She stood there with her eyes closed and then said softly, "I was so afraid..."

"Afraid?" Danni said very softly.

Tracy opened her eyes. "I was afraid for Colleen—Colleen is...well, you must know how amazing she is. And how trusting. I was afraid she trusted the wrong person. Of course, you two are very old friends, but I hadn't seen you, didn't know you until the other day.... I mean, we don't know everything about

Colleen, except that she's so sweet and giving...and I'm rambling because this is so very horrible."

"How did you get here without seeing what was going on?" Danni asked.

Trent pointed behind them and to the right. "I own a lot of land around here. I was showing Tracy one of my hunting lodges. It borders the cemetery. This place is...well, gone to hell, but very historic. The first burials here were in 1779—right after the area was settled. In the 1800s, the Victorian era brought some beautiful funerary art...I just wanted to show Tracy my little lodge, and then we were there, so...I thought I should show her the cemetery. We..." he paused, wincing, "we had no idea anything had happened."

Danni nodded; she hadn't seen them this morning at the lodge. She didn't know if that meant maybe they'd spent the night at Trent Anderson's more private lodge, or she just hadn't seen them. She didn't know if Trent had even taken a room at Honeywell Lodge since he was a local; he had been at the first mixer where he'd been very popular and wore an air of confidence as easily as he wore his designer suit. He was a good-looking man, tall, with a wave of dark hair that fell over one of his deep green eyes.

And of course, he was very wealthy—which couldn't hurt.

"Danni?"

She was grateful to hear Quinn calling her name. He came around the curve of the grassy-sloped tombs, a worried frown on his face. He stopped dead before he reached her, looking curiously at Trent and Tracy.

"Quinn, I think you met Trent and Tracy last night," Danni said quickly. "Trent has a lodge right over there," she said, pausing to point, "and they were just here because Trent is local and knows the area so well. He wanted Tracy to see the historic cemetery." No one said anything, so she continued. "Tracy is Colleen's office manager in New York and Trent is..."

Her voice trailed; she had just said he was local. "Trent was part of the little opening party last night. I think you met then. I think we all met...everyone who was there."

"Yes, of course," Quinn said, stepping forward to shake Trent's hand. The man immediately responded.

"We were just sitting here. I had been telling Tracy these are some of the oldest tombs" He scrunched his face into a wry grimace. "Weird, I know, but I've always been fascinated by the history of this place. I grew up around here—thought I knew it through and through, but to be honest, I didn't realize there was an opening hole—until I saw Danni coming out just now," Trent said.

Quinn looked at Danni, lightly arching a brow. He didn't speak his question to her aloud, but she knew what he was silently wondering.

What the heck were you doing? Where were you exactly?

"Ah," he said to Trent and Tracy. "Well, I imagine all kinds of secrets have been well-kept by nature around here," he said. "Of course, the situation right now means you really shouldn't be here. I don't know how long the police will have the immediate area cordoned off, but I don't believe anyone knew there were people in the cemetery."

"We didn't know!" Tracy said. "It's so horrible."

"We've been out and hadn't heard the news this morning," Trent continued.

"No news," Tracy repeated.

"Well, I'm sure this will be all over every form of media very soon," Quinn said. He glanced at Danni again. "So...um, let's walk these two past the police so they don't wind up having to stop to answer all kinds of questions again."

Danni hesitated. Tracy might not have been best friends with Ally Caldwell, but she had known her. It was hard enough to see what they had seen, the mangled bodies set up like scarecrows, but to see a friend or an acquaintance so...

"The M.E. and his assistants have moved on out," he said quietly.

"Okay," Danni murmured. "We can walk you through—"

"My car is on the other side of the little hammock by the cemetery," Trent said.

"Well, then," Quinn said, "we'll stroll with you. You can show us your property. I guess you just walked over a bit of broken wall."

"Easy as pie," Tracy said.

As they walked, Quinn wasn't cheerful, but he was polite. He was obviously interested in Trent Anderson. "Local. I guess you know all the local legends."

"Oh, yeah, there's Yvette and the thing about women getting murdered every few decades. But of course, not sweet, beautiful women like you," he told Tracy, and then remembered that her co-worker had just been murdered. "Oh, I'm sorry. How terrible of me, I didn't mean...you asked about legend.

Half the world has a 'Bloody Mary' story and for us, it's Yvette. I didn't mean...Tracy, I am so sorry!"

"It's okay, it's okay—I didn't see Ally every day. We were in the same offices, but she was gone a lot and when we were in, she was in her office and I'm always right outside Colleen's office, and I guess Colleen usually went to her office when they were discussing business...I mean, it's truly horrible, and of course, we're all effected by it, but...sad to say, she wasn't my best friend or even a close one. I just keep sounding worse and worse, don't I? I am so sorry—and, of course, it's terrifying, and Colleen must be devastated, but...oh, there you go. Ally was a workaholic. She didn't come down from New York to New Orleans with us, she came on her own. When a group of us made our arrangements for a van to come out, she wasn't ready, she wanted a car of her own."

"How did she get her car? You're the office manager. Did you order it for her?"

Tracy shook her head. "I asked Colleen if I was supposed to order a separate car for her, but Colleen said arrangements were already made."

"We'll find out about the car company—could be her driver who was with her, in the cemetery and...with her," Quinn finished a little awkwardly.

"Dead! She was dead, in the cemetery, not far from us! We were just lying back on that little mound and talking and...oh!" Tracy said.

Trent put an arm around her shoulders as they walked. "I'm so sorry. What idiot brings a woman to a cemetery?" he apologized.

"No idiot," she said, touching his face lightly but with adoring eyes, "just a great man who knows history and nature are amazing!"

Danni looked over at Quinn. He was watching the two, perplexed.

When the couple were a bit ahead of them, he asked, "Were we ever that...creepy?" he asked.

She smiled. "Um, so much for the romance of it all, huh?"

"Oh, wait, I forgot. I thought you were a spoiled party girl, and you thought I was a terrible jerk. Well, once upon a time, I was a jerk. Still...is that romance?"

"I'm guessing it depends on who you are," Danni said. She maneuvered around a broken headstone barely visible in the long grass.

"So, where were you—in a vault? Alone? In a cemetery where two murders just took place?"

"I was within ear shot of you, Larue, Ellsworth, and a half dozen parish workers," she said. But she looked at him, remembering, "Quinn, you've got to get down there. There are five or so coffins...well, sarcophagi or tombs with coffins in them, but there are bones all over the floor—and the coffins are filled with straw."

He stared at her. "And you didn't tell me this right away?"

"You were talking about legends! People around us, remember?"

He winced. "Yeah, yeah, sorry, but..."

He walked quickly, twisting somewhat as he did so. The cemetery had not been laid out with a designer's hand; trails appeared and disappeared. All manner of stone filled the place, along with the few vaults and dozens of the "city of the dead" style family mausoleums. Then there were cherubs, lambs, angels, and other artistic memorials, some in better shape than others.

It occurred to her that the place must be incredibly eerie and sad by night. She'd lived in New Orleans all her life; she knew well what many referred to as the "decaying elegance" of the NOLA cities of the dead.

This place...

It was more. So many burial styles, so many chipped and broken tombs and stones. Age sitting upon the place like a gray and dismal aura.

Danni suddenly felt as if something had wound around her ankle. Shrubbery! The place was so overgrown!

She fought to steady herself, but she could not—she pitched forward, stopping herself from meeting with the ground by catching the edge of a life-sized child holding a lamb. Luckily she had caught herself just before she could fall on a chipped and decaying tombstone.

The last name was all but obliterated, but she could read the first name.

Yvette.

Chapter 4

Quinn looked back to see Danni bent over, clutching an old and broken tombstone. He frowned as he saw her face; she was wearing a very strange expression, but as he started to head back toward her, she shook her head slightly. Whatever it was, she didn't want to share with Trent and Tracy, and the two had paused just feet ahead of him.

He waited for her to straighten and head their way, smiling and apologizing. "Tripped! But I'm fine. Caught myself." She extended a hand toward the expanse of land they were approaching. They had almost reached the remnants of the old stone wall and beyond; it seemed trees and foliage stretched forever—the earth was rich here, marshy and wet, and greenery took hold in abundance.

"That's all yours?" she said to Trent. "Lovely!"

Trent laughed. "Yes, it's all mine. I do love my home. To be honest—all my acres out here are equivalent to one mansion in the Garden District.New Orleans is surely one of the most beautiful and continental cities in the country, but this is home."

"The area is fascinating," Danni said. "Where's your lodge?"

Trent pointed through the trees. "Believe it or not, there's a little trail."

"It never...freaked you out, when you were a kid, to be so close to a cemetery, huh?" Tracy asked him, wide-eyed.

Trent grinned. "It was just always here. I loved the stories—and having kids out for weekends when I could take them into the cemetery and tell them all the wild stories." He lost his smile. "I would have never thought...well, someone would use them or...kill people." His voice grew low and somber. "Our stories were all about lonely ghosts—not the living murdering one another."

They stood at the old wall for a few awkward moments.

"What about Yvette?" Quinn asked. "Lonely—but murdered—seeking revenge?"

Trent laughed. "Yvette, Mary, Kathy, Pam...every decent old cemetery has a broken-hearted lover. Or a vengeful ghost." He sobered quickly. "I'm sorry—I forgot. People are dead." He seemed to realize he was standing in a cemetery and he winced. "Newly dead. I'm so sorry—we have lots of legends and lore and most places have violence in their past histories, but...we're small. Really, bad things don't happen here that often anymore."

"I'm sure," Danni murmured, and they all stood in silence for a minute.

"We need to get moving," Tracy said nervously, "get the car, and get back to Honeywell Lodge. Colleen will be going crazy. She won't have Ally; she'll be devastated. She'll need me. And I...well, I suppose we must go on. We have a lodge that's filled with people, and most of them never knew Ally—she tended to be business behind the scenes. Oh...I don't want to go back! Poor Colleen!"

"She will need you," Danni said. "She'll need all the support she can get."

"I'd love to see your place, sometime," Quinn told Trent.

"Sure. Whenever...ah, whenever you can," Trent said.

Quinn slipped an arm around Danni as they watched them go. They could barely see the two as they walked along the trail. Just flashes of color here and there. When they were out of view and earshot, Quinn turned anxiously to Danni.

"What happened?"

"Nothing," she said, looking at him with brilliant blue eyes, a slight flush on her cheeks. "I tripped, honestly. But caught myself—for real. What I tripped over though was a stone with the name Yvette on it—can't read the last name anymore. And Quinn, I'm sure a tombstone can't be causing this...if you go by legend—and maybe even records!—bad things only happen every few decades. That may just be the natural way of life, and then any bad thing can be chalked up to...legends and curses or superstition."

He shook his head. "Not a stone."

"What? You think the murders might have been caused by a—tombstone?" she asked skeptically. "You think this is something more than...just a crazy person committing heinous murders?"

"One of the CSIs is local—there are several legends. That of Yvette and her spirit, I suppose, ridding the world of evil women, and another about settlers who first came to this area. The woman was a witch and she killed her husband and a friend, or something like that, but supposedly it was because of some kind of talisman that caused a person to go insane. I don't know—it's all stories at the moment, but..."

He paused. He'd met her not long after her father's death when they'd had to find and destroy an ancient statue, because it apparently did very bad things. That any such thing could be true had been a massive shock to her. Quinn was certain Angus, tough old massive Scot the man had been, never intended to leave his daughter unaware—and vulnerable. But he had.

It didn't take long for her to come to understand, which was very good, because their next case had involved an extremely evil painting from the summer when Mary Shelley had penned *Frankenstein*, and then a saxophone—charmed, cursed, or not—and they'd dealt with a wicked doll, and even the rougarou.

Now, after all they'd been through, while he might be the P.I., there was no way she wasn't going to plunge in; it was what they did.

"Library—parish library!" Danni said. "I'll have to see what I can dig up there. But Quinn, Larue is out here because of a similar crime scene in NOLA?"

"Yes. So...I don't know. Maybe the killer is local—and just needed to dispatch someone in NOLA, too. Or maybe...at this point, who knows? Maybe the murderer has already moved on, and we'll hear about such a case in Baton Rouge or...Texas. Right now..."

"I'll start with the local legends," Danni said.

"All right. The doc is going to start the autopsies as soon as he gets the corpses in and cleaned up. I'll be with Larue and Ellsworth at the morgue. I'll get you to the library first. When the killer realizes you have a talent for finding out what shouldn't be known..."

"I have a feeling this killer will be happy; he wants it all chalked up to legend," Danni said. "Maybe. We have to get back to the lodge, too, right after. But first..."

"First, where's this Yvette who tripped you? And after that..."

"After that?"

"Your cave or tomb entry. But we'll start with Yvette."

Danni smiled, "Come meet her. It's an old stone, not a big tomb or mausoleum grave. Just a stone. At some time, though, someone must have re-etched the first name."

"Well, Yvette...every school kid around here has heard about Yvette, so I understand. Not to mention the fact this cemetery might well hold dozens who went by the name of Yvette when they were living."

"So, tell me, before I start the research—when I find out about people who might have offed one another because of an object, what do you think I'm looking for?"

"A charm or a talisman...something small enough for someone to carry. It's supposed to cause insanity and murderous rages, and sometimes, suicide as well. I guess it depends on just how mad you are at yourself."

Danni studied him. "Do you think there is such a thing? The legend seems to come from here—and while New Orleans is huge at Halloween, I don't remember celebrating a lot of harvest festivals when I was growing up."

"No. But I haven't had a chance to talk to Larue about the murders in New Orleans yet—the concentration has been about Ally Caldwell here—and whoever the man with her may be. Where's your Yvette?" he asked.

"This a-way," she said, turning to lead. He followed her back along the trail with its overgrown grass, weeds and occasional flowers, almost tripping over a broken stone on the ground himself.

He could see right away when she stopped that she had been right; everything on the stone was obliterated—other than the first name, Yvette.

"And you think she reached out and grabbed you?" he asked Danni, only halfway teasing.

"No, I think I tripped. Caught my foot in some weeds. It was just...ironic, I guess. Though, in this cemetery, I believe you are probably right. There will be dozens of stones with the name Yvette on them."

He nodded. "Onward—to your secret entry to the vaults!"

"It's not a secret, just low to the ground and covered over with some bracken."

Again, she turned, and they started back to the vaults that were half underground, and half built up high above it.

"Three," Quinn noted.

Danni nodded gravely. "So, we have three hills, three scarecrows, well, three in New Orleans, and three out here. The vaults may just be happenstance."

He indicated he'd like to lead on the way in. He drew a penlight from his pocket and played it around the dank vault walls as he leapt down to the earth floor of the vault. Shining his light around, he saw there had been walls constructed of concrete and brick down here; he imagined the vaults had once been higher above the ground, but time had sunk them as deep as they were, with time building up the "roofs" of the tombs and nature taking over to make them appear to be hills.

Danni hopped down beside him. "There's a straight line of a narrow tunnel leading from one of these to the next," she said. "Quinn, it's so bizarre—all the coffins or tombs in here are filled with straw. Whoever originally lay in each coffin has been removed. If you look around, there are bones everywhere littering the floor."

It was as she said, bones haphazardly lying about everywhere.

"A year and a day," he murmured, referring to the time the intense heat of the Louisiana sun took to rapidly decompose and cremate a body naturally when it was in a coffin, on a stone slab, in a crypt until only the bones were left. It was the time a family had to wait before the remains of the loved one could be shoveled into a holding container at the end of a crypt thus allowing space for another family member to be buried within the tomb. Which was why there could be so many names on a tomb that might appear only large enough for six coffins.

Family might really join with family in the holding containers that held the naturally cremated ash and the bones.

But this was different from most of the family crypts or mausoleums in the famous cemeteries of New Orleans. These had been the same, perhaps once standing higher in the cemetery. But shelves for those interred had not been against the walls and arranged for most space. Rather, concrete sarcophagi had been built to house coffins in the middle of the floor.

He headed to the first; it was indeed filled with straw.

He quickly looked in two other coffins in the crypt.

Straw.

"What do you make of it?" Danni asked.

He shook his head. "I have no idea. The straw might have been here a long time...and our murderer just knew about it. The way the bones are strewn about and broken...I think the tomb was rifled some time ago." He shrugged, looking around the dark, damp, and eerie space. "We all know teenagers like to party in tombs, but..."

"No beer cans, no cigarette butts—no sign kids came here to fool around," Danni said.

"No, I will bet our killer did come here for his straw—whether he brought it or found it out here. We need to know who these tombs were for—that might mean something," Quinn said.

He raised his light and looked to the side and saw the narrow opening that was something of an earth tunnel from this crypt to the next. Danni followed him. In the next two vaults, they found the same thing.

Empty coffins, bones littered everywhere.

"No jewelry, no belt buckles, no buttons," Quinn said.

"You think grave robbers at some time?"

Quinn nodded. "Someone had to have been buried with something. We'll get the crime scene investigators in here—see if they can find anything. It seems to me this place has really been stripped of anything that might have had some value."

"But why straw?" Danni asked. "Unless you know you're going to create a human scarecrow."

"Why, indeed?" Quinn murmured. "Let's head out—I need to get you to the library. And I need to get to the autopsy—and talk to Jake Larue."

They made their way back through the second tomb. As they re-entered the first, they heard a loud, startled gasp.

Larue was down in the tomb, staring at them as if they were the walking dead.

He swore softly. "Holy Mother of God!" he exclaimed. "Where the hell?"

"Two more of these, exactly the same," Quinn told him.

Larue shook his head. "I think you just cost me a decade of life. I didn't see...where the hell, how the hell..."

"There's a bit of a tunnel connecting this one to the next, and then to the next," Quinn explained.

"And the others?" Larue asked.

"Just like this. Ellsworth is local—he may know more about these crypts," Quinn said. "We'll send the techs down here and get to the morgue with Ellsworth."

"Weird. I mean, I've come to know weird hanging around with you," Larue said, "But this is...weird." He lifted his hands suddenly. "And if you find out these murders were committed by an intellectually advanced rougarou or the like, don't tell me—I don't want to know!"

"No. There's someone human involved in this, I assure you," Quinn said.

Larue sighed. "Isn't there always?" he asked. "Monsters, yeah. The real ones come in flesh and blood. Human flesh and blood."

***

Perryville was a tiny town. It had a tiny library.

There were only two librarians, Mrs. Beauvoir, the woman at the check-out counter told Danni, beaming and delighted as they chatted. She was a petite woman with salt-and-pepper hair, thrilled, it seemed, to be talking to anyone.

"We do stay open seven days a week!" she said proudly. "Nine in the morning until seven. Mrs. Flowers—Genevieve— and I share the time, three and a half days and three and a half days. And over time, we've collected an amazing array of books. Of course, the kids come in and head straight to the computers these days, but our books are fantastic!"

Danni explained she was looking into local history and legends, and Mrs. Beauvoir sighed deeply. "I heard! Horrible murders—in the cemetery no less. All the stories about Yvette will start up again, and...well, with that new place opened by that lovely young woman, Colleen Rankin, we will have more tourism. Oh well, we always get some good local trade during harvest time—there's a big fair going on now, you know! Harvest time—it's how many of the shopkeepers survive all year. Oh, you must find time to get to the harvest festival. Runs two weeks; there are rides, animal shows, and contests for the local children."

"Nice," Danni murmured.

She didn't want to be rude; she wanted to study the history of the area and see what she could find out about Yvette. Discover if she had been real—and see if there was anything that suggested scarecrows should come in threes—especially three as in dead people, but she listened politely, and courtesy paid off.

Mrs. Beauvoir led her into an archive room where they kept their oldest records and books. "We have church records from a number of the first churches here, too—some in buildings that, sadly, went the way of time. You'll love it! We even have diaries in there, along with records. Now usually, we don't let anyone in there, but...you're trying to help the police, right? And you're such a sweet thing!"

Danni smiled at that, not sure she was happy to be a sweet "thing." But Mrs. Beauvoir was a sweet little "thing," too, and Danni was grateful she was being allowed into the little library's most sacred and climate-controlled room.

Mrs. Beauvoir left her, excited because the local grade school was having a special day. She was going to be working with thirty students, helping teach the French and Acadian history of the area, and showing off work done by local authors through the years.

Danni headed to work, taking a minute to study the little room. It was about twenty feet by twenty feet, with a large desk in the center and rows of well-ordered record books and file boxes.

Her heart sank a little as she realized just how many years of records she might have to examine, but to her delight, as she glanced into one of the file boxes, she saw personal diaries were among the finds which had been carefully preserved.

She read an introductory sheet in the first diary she picked up; it had been written by a bride coming to the area in 1889 with her husband. Danni thought she needed to go further back, but she quickly glanced over the information the young bride had written.

People had first settled around Bayou Teche in the late 1770s, but Acadians had travelled to the area in small numbers even earlier, forced south because of the French and Indian wars with the British. Then came the American Revolution, but by then...

Over time, English and Americans had come, and then people from just about everywhere. Still, through the years, the area remained heavily "Cajun," the word being a bastardization of *Acadian.*

The bride, Danni noted, had married a man named Beauvoir—possibly an antecedent of the librarian?

She smiled and looked on.

After looking through several of the boxes, she found a leather-bound diary neatly secreted into one; it was dated 1811, and the journal-keeper had been a young woman named Yvette.

The first pages were heart-breaking. There were days in which Yvette carefully penned in her first meetings with the handsome and dashing young Percival. She saw him at the harvest festival, where all members of the community gathered, forgetting their ethnic differences. Percival was charming, and she knew how he cared for her.

Throughout the year, she spoke of her love. She spoke of their time together, and then...

He asked her to marry him.

It was at the harvest festival; all had gathered together again, celebrating with rich platters of food, with prayers that made the people one. They even gathered together to create scarecrows

Danni felt her stomach clench as she read on.

Each year, they saw to it scarecrows were set in the fields. Three for each farmer. It had not been an Acadian tradition, but it had been brought by the English or American settlers. That was because, hundreds of years before, in a small town in Northern Britain, a famine had caused many in the village there to starve. A pagan priestess had decreed the land was angry, and asked for the cycle to come anew, birth, life, and death. Sacrifices were demanded. Human sacrifices. So, two men and one woman had been chosen, and they had been tied to poles, their throats slashed, and the land had been fed. The next year the harvest was rich, but in memory, every year three scarecrows were set in each field and they were especially fashioned for the harvest festival, warding off hunger, evil spirits, and any further need for blood.

Christianity had come to Europe; but for certain small communities, the need for three scarecrows to honor the harvest remained.

"No human sacrifices here," she murmured. "At least...not as far as Yvette knew?"

She carried the diary to the desk, noting there weren't many more pages. As she sat, she wondered if this was the

Yvette supposedly murdered by the woman who would have been her mother-in-law.

And was that why her story soon stopped?

She thought it might have been.

Yvette went on to write, "So tonight! Beneath the harvest moon, Percival told me we were betrothed, and he did not care what anyone said or thought—we would go away. We would build our lives far from this place where it did not matter what a man or a woman's birth might be. I love him so much. He is passionate. He is kind and merciful to those around him, and he has no patience with those who would be French or English. He provides work for the Italians and Spanish who are also coming this way. He is the best man. I love him more than life itself."

More than life itself.

That was Yvette's final entry.

***

"There's an historic house right on the line where the City of New Orleans meets Metairie," Larue said. "It's called the MacDonald Mansion, after the old soldier who built it there soon after the Revolutionary War. Guess he was a Scot who had taken part in some of the rebellions back home. After the war, he just decided to stay in the new country. Anyway, at the time, he had a lot of acreage and so he had a family cemetery built on the property with a little chapel. There were a few mausoleums built, and there are a few in-ground graves as well. Nothing special or fancy, but about twenty years ago, the family opened the house—a lot of history there, of course. General Beauregard took it over for some of his men during the Civil War, so you have a few Civil War burials and interments there as well. Anyway...only one family member is living there now, a young Fiona MacDonald, and she's up in the attic. The house has an alarm system, but no security cameras. Last night, I was called out because there had been two homicides, and..."

"Two people, sliced up, displayed as scarecrows—and a third man already dead?" Quinn asked.

Larue nodded gravely. "The woman was a tourist—she'd only been in the city a week. Her name was Belinda Cardigan. The man was a local—Leon Grissom, a drunk, but apparently well liked by those around him, friends who tried to get him help all the time. He had some bruises—as if he might have been picked for the honor because he tried to help Miss Cardigan."

"And the corpse?" Quinn asked.

"Kenneth Brown, a man interred in his family tomb just last week. The killer was careful not to disturb the tomb from the outside. Inside, the broken concrete is everywhere. Anyway, now, it makes less sense than ever. It's harvest time—not a big deal in NOLA like Halloween and Christmas, though it might be out here in the country. There's got to be some whacky, really sick thing dredged out of the past. Scarecrows! Go figure. Ritual...something," Larue said, shaking his head. "I just want to know how the hell it's something that happened out here—and back in New Orleans!"

"I wish you would have called me last night. It would have helped if I had been there at the first scene."

"I wanted you and Danni to have a vacation. A free vacation." He sighed. "Father Ryan called me, Billie called me, Natasha called me...we all agreed you needed your vacation, and as of last night, nothing suggested it was going to be..."

"Going to be?" Quinn pressed.

Larue sighed. "I was going to say 'weird.' But there's no way out of these being very weird cases. Weird cases that border on...weirder stuff!" Larue said. "Here's the thing—it's all Louisiana, southern Louisiana, to be precise. French, Acadian influence. But NOLA is like a little United Nations. When you get out into the rural areas and the bayou region, it's different. People think of themselves as different. So, what could cause this kind of murder right in NOLA—and then out here?"

"What might the victims have in common?" Quinn murmured.

"The two already-dead men couldn't have had anything in common—I don't think. And Allison Caldwell was a big-shot business woman, attractive, but—from all accounts—something of a witch. My female victim back in NOLA, Belinda Cardigan, was apparently well-liked. She was on her way through the city, she told the manager at her bed and breakfast inn. She paid right away, she smiled, and told her just how wonderful she found the city to be. Nice, friendly—and she was a nurse. Hardly a high-powered business woman. There's no way to find similarities on the newly dead men since we still don't have an identity on the murdered man at Ally's side," Larue paused, shaking his head. He closed his eyes.

Quinn was glad he was the one doing the driving as they headed to the parish morgue.

"I think there are still several weeks left that might be considered 'harvest time,'" Larue said. "If this is some crazy ritual killer..."

"That's possible," Quinn said. "But..."

"But, what? The young crime scene investigator said there was a legend about a witchy woman going crazy and killing people because of a talisman. Weird, that she killed everyone and then herself. Impossible, as we noted, to string your own dead body up on a pole. So, if the legend is anywhere near true, someone else was involved. Punishment for someone not-so-nice? Sure, kill a woman who is torturing those around her, one way or another. I mean—that's motive. But, digging up corpses? This really makes no sense at all, but since I know you and Danni, if you think there is a talisman...well, we can dig up every damned bone in the place if you think it's necessary!"

"Legends." Quinn glanced at Larue, then back to the road. "Yes, there could be some kind of talisman or object involved, and whether its power is real or imagined and expected, it doesn't really matter if someone wants to use it to commit murder. Thing is, I can't help it. I don't think these murders were random."

"What could the connection be? Just the crazy killer!" Larue said. "He doesn't seem to be choosing a type. Belinda Cardigan was a pretty, well-liked blond. Ally Caldwell had hair that was almost black, and she was known to be hell on wheels. I'm thinking both victims were handy; they happened to be where the killer needed them when he needed them."

Quinn shrugged and glanced at Larue. "One way or the other, we have to get a handle on this—quickly. As you said, there are weeks left in the harvest season. And, my God, do we ever have more venues for such a display in Louisiana, more cities, all with cemeteries, graveyards and churchyards, hundreds of them in the state—and beyond. Many old and decaying—"

"Just waiting for a few scarecrows for some harvest decoration!" Larue said glumly. "Quinn, I'm thinking I need to get back home. I've seen this now—"

"I need to get to New Orleans, too. There—and back," Quinn said. "I definitely need to be back here as soon as possible. There's about to be a harvest ball and..."

"And?"

"I have a very bad feeling about it. A very, very bad feeling," Quinn said.

He had a feeling it wasn't going to happen that day—night was already falling.

Night...

Darkness.

All conducive to another kill.

Chapter 5

"I don't know what we're going to do—I just don't know what we're going to do," Larry Blythe, Colleen's business manager said.

He wasn't in tears, but definitely seemed on the verge. He was nervously running his fingers up and down his coffee cup as he sat with Danni in the little café toward the entry to the lodge. She was trying to ask him questions. He was, she thought, a naturally nervous little man. Not really little—she was fairly tall, about five-ten, and it seemed he was smaller than she was. Not that other men weren't sometimes, but he was also thin, wore thin-framed glasses, and simply had a nervous look about him.

She set a hand on his, trying to calm, or assure him.

"You just don't understand," he said. "I mean, Ally...she had brains, you know. Yes, yes, you'll hear people say she was a bitch, but not really—it was just her way. Her mind was always working, you know? She could come up with facts and figures like no one else—and when Colleen wanted something believed in, Ally could put that vision together for her. Colleen, she...well, if it weren't for me and Ally, she'd still be dreaming her dreams, because her heart is huge—but her head for finances is almost non-existent!" He stopped speaking long enough to shake his head and stare at her, frowning. "You're not a cop. I heard you're an artist who owns a shop on Royal Street in New Orleans. The Charmed Puppy, or something like that."

"Cheshire Cat," Danni said, "and—"

"Colleen wanted to buy a lot of your art for this place," he said. He shook his head again, and then his eyes widened. "Oh, you're married to a cop, that big guy!"

"We aren't married, and Quinn isn't a cop. He is a private investigator."

"Oh. oh," he said, looking at her as if it should have explained her questions, but it just didn't really.

"I do a lot of research and interviewing for Quinn."

"And," he said, his voice sounding strangled, "you're going to find out what happened to our Ally!" He moved closer to her. "It's a rite—or voodoo. These people out here—they're very strange. I've heard they're different. They're not like people in cities. They're voodoo people who raise the devil or something like that."

"Mr. Blythe, I have friends in the city who practice voodoo, and please believe me, they're very good people who would never hurt anyone," Danni said.

"Right. Sure."

He didn't believe her.

"So, not voodoo. Another weird cult. Pagans or Satanists. They did it. They killed our Ally."

"Larry, right now, we don't know who killed Ally—and that's why we need everyone's help."

"Help. Yes, of course, I'll help you. I wish I could help you. That's just it—Ally was always working. The rest of us, we headed out here—from NOLA—together. We were all here in the afternoon, getting ready for last night's mixer. But no, Ally had to check on some future gig she wanted to talk to us about once she got here, and now...she's ruined everything!" he finished in a whisper.

Danni arched her brows, surprised by his words. "Larry, I hardly think she was murdered, slashed horribly, on purpose."

"Oh, God!" he said stricken. "I didn't mean it the way it sounded at all! I meant, her being murdered...I mean, for Ally of course. It's heart-breaking. But this is also huge for Colleen. I mean, first of all, she had Trent Anderson here. That meant so much. I mean the idea is you could have chatted online, and then seen one another face to face here, in a safe place. Or, you could come to one of Colleen's lodges, see someone, and then chat them up online. I mean, she's right. Even if you're perfect for each other on a piece of paper, it doesn't mean the chemistry will mix or that you'll even like each other!"

"Yes, of course," Danni murmured. "I understand all of that, but I'm trying very hard to discover—did anyone know anything about the car that picked Ally up to bring her out here?"

He shook his head. "You had to have known Ally. She was as independent as a curse! She'd snap at you if you tried to help. She did things as she wanted. She and I were both the business end of things—along with Albert Bennett. Albert always arranged for security—on the computer, and when we're setting things up for an event like this." He brightened suddenly. "Maybe Albert knows something—he and Ally..."

"He and Ally...what?" Danni pursued.

"It's not my place," Larry said.

"Please, Larry, Ally is dead. Anything you can say..."

He shook his head. "It's over all ready. She was found in the cemetery. Up on a pole like a scarecrow with another man and a...corpse! And another murder right before—in New Orleans! This has to be some kind of a crazy cult killing. Me talking about my co-workers isn't going to help anything."

"Larry, please—it honestly could help."

He sighed, looking around nervously. Danni knew she had to go and see Colleen again and help in any way she could, but she was trying to speak with Colleen's top people first.

She'd already seen Tracy Willard—in the cemetery. She needed to speak with Albert Bennett, but perhaps it was important to hear what Larry had to say about him, first.

"I don't really know anything," he said, "but sometimes, when I'd see them together, I'd think there was something going on between them. I think..." he paused awkwardly. Then without her prompting, he continued in a rush, "Ally was strange in many ways. She was always moving forward—she'd hitched her wagon to a star, she believed, and she was going to push it all the way, become rich herself. Ally didn't need to be famous—just rich. I think sex might have been like breathing to her—something necessary now and then...and Albert is a good-looking guy."

"What did Colleen think?"

"Colleen only sees the good in people. She's oblivious." He sighed deeply again. "I might be wrong. Tracy liked to flirt with Albert, too."

"Was Ally jealous?"

"God, no. Like I said. Sex was just a physical function, needed now and then. Then again, when I'd see Tracy with some of our clients, I'd think there was something going on there, too."

Danni stayed quiet. She believed Tracy had been doing more than flirting with Trent Anderson.

"Thank you, Larry."

"But, you see what I mean? Office dynamics could have had nothing to do with this. Perryville is certainly a weird little town, and I'd bet this is some kind of crazy thing out of New Orleans. Scarecrows tend to be more in the countryside, but crazy—that's New Orleans." He was talking about her city. Yes, it could be crazy, but there were so many beautiful and wonderful things about the city, too, she couldn't help but take offense at his tone.

"Trust me," she murmured. "Crazy can be anywhere."

He didn't seem to hear her; he was looking toward the counter.

"Oh, there's Albert, if you want to talk to him—I can go get him. Oh, you won't say I said anything, will you?"

Danni looked to the counter. Albert Bennett was ordering coffee, offering the young girl behind the counter a flashing white smile.

He was a big man, and an arresting one. She could easily see how he might have charmed both Ally and Tracy Willard.

"I'm fine; I'll ask him if we might talk," Danni said. She didn't want to question him with Larry Blythe present. She wanted to hear what he had to say for himself.

"Well, good, I have work to do—we're checking in with all our clients, trying to assure them Ally got caught in a mess that has nothing to do with the weekend. Of course, we're all broken-heartened, but as sad as the situation is, they don't need to leave. We'll be going on as we planned."

After Larry took his leave, Danni walked to the counter. Albert Bennett, handsome in a perfectly tailored suit, looked at her and offered her a smile. "Danni! How are you doing?"

"I'm fine, thank you. I didn't know Ally. This must be devastating for you, though."

"A non-fat latte, Mr. Bennett," the girl behind the counter said. She studied Danni, and looked like she was trying to decide if Danni was someone in authority or if she might be competition for the man's attention.

Whichever, she turned away.

"Albert, would you sit down with me for a minute?" she asked.

He looked at her somewhat surprised, but said, "My pleasure. Certainly."

Apparently, he thought she was flirting—even though he had seen her with Quinn.

"I have a number of duties to attend to—complicated by events, but," he told her, and winked, "I always have a few minutes for a beautiful woman, especially one who is an old friend of the boss!" He pulled out a chair for her at one of the café tables, adding, "I'd rather thought you were with Mr. Very Tall and Muscled last night—Flynn...Finn...can't recall exactly, but he had the look of a cop or maybe FBI."

"Neither, and his name is Quinn. He's a private investigator, and yes, we're together," Danni said.

He had taken his seat, but the look on his face then denoted that he didn't know why. He was clearly wasting his time.

"Mr. Bennett," she said, getting right to it, "I'd like to ask you about Allison Caldwell, Ally."

He looked surprised—and then guarded.

"She's dead; we learned that this morning. Horribly murdered in that old derelict cemetery by some crazy cult or wiccan or voodoo person or persons."

"You don't seem very upset about a co-worker," she said.

He sighed. "I'm upset. And the way it was done...but you didn't know Ally."

"I'm sorry, what does that mean?"

His expression was pained, and he frowned quizzically as he looked down, and then up at her.

"Why are you...? I mean, I talked to cops this morning, you know. We all did. You're an artist, right, not a cop? You know— you could be an artist's model, if you're not...I mean, if Colleen was buying things just because you are her friend. Oh, wow, that didn't come out right at all, I'm afraid. Well, the situation is a mess. I just mean you're attractive...sleek, elegant, still natural...you'd make a good model. I don't want to mess with Mr. Very Tall and Muscular Quinn—it's an observation, nothing more."

"Thank you. Yes, I'm an artist, a decent artist. I do many local scenes, and I'm sure the fact I'm friends with Colleen made her think of my work, but I'm just trying to help Quinn out a bit here, chatting with people, seeing if anything will help. So, please, tell me, what did you mean by telling me I didn't know Ally?"

He appeared to be pained again. "You're not supposed to speak ill of the dead," he murmured.

"Did you have an affair with her?"

"Affair?" He asked, offering a dry and crooked smile. "Ally didn't have affairs."

"So, no."

"No, I never had an affair with her. Did I sleep with her? Yes. A few times, but...sex was like a business deal with her. No foreplay, no small talk. A business deal. Sign on the dotted line, and you're done. She was a huge fan of another dating site—one with a title that spelled it all out—*Quickie.* You could really just walk by someone and see if they wanted sex then, just then, no names needed, go for it and done. That was Ally. There was something...something missing in her. What I meant was if she had gotten into something with someone local—say a killer just looking for a random victim—he might have thought she was a great person to off. She could be downright rude."

Danni looked at him, nodding slowly. He seemed sincere. He wasn't trying to look away from her; he wanted her to understand.

"Did that hurt you?" she asked.

He shook his head. "I knew her—I knew exactly what she wanted. She was a pretty woman, built nicely...sex was casual. For her—and for me. She knew it would be over for me if I did meet someone, while..."

"While?"

"While she was never looking for someone. And she'd have never found anyone. She didn't want a relationship or children. She was...different. Oh, huh. I did forget one thing."

"What's that?"

"Maybe nothing, but..."

"But, please, what?"

He shrugged. "I'm not pulling this out of my hat—we talked now and then." He grimaced. "Not during sex or anything, but just about the site, the future, and our own feelings on things. She was clear she didn't want marriage or baggage, that her career and her own determination on her future were key in her life. But now and then she did express interest in a client. You know, casual things when we were vetting people for the site. Yes, she'd take a tumble with this man or someone being good looking. She did tell me looks didn't count for all that much in bed, but why try out ugly merchandise? She said once she did have an interest in meeting a man who would be here for this event. Colleen's big 'coup,' more or less. That rich guy—he was here last night. Trent Anderson. Definitely interested in a tumble, and if he didn't smell bad or have rotten teeth, she would consider marriage. She said with his kind of money, she'd think about it. Even if she married him for a year or two and got a divorce. That kind of money, well, it could buy a hell of a lot."

"She'd never met him in person?"

"Not that I know of—we all just met him last night."

"I see," Danni said.

"Hey, I attract women. But that guy—they were all over him last night like bees on honey. I guess he's the whole package—and he didn't seem to smell. Not that I got close."

"So, she never met him, and no one knew last night she was...being murdered."

"I guess not. Was she murdered during our event?"

"I don't know," Danni said honestly. "She was found just this morning."

"You should talk to him," Bennett said.

"Yes." She didn't say she already had—that she'd met up with him in the cemetery where Ally's body had been strung up.

She asked, "Did you order the car for her? Your job is security—don't you make sure the companies you worked with are vetted?"

"I do. But I didn't order the car for her. She was angry when the rest of us tried to help her—she said she'd take care of things herself." He pursed his lips and shook his head suddenly. "I wish I could help you. I really wish I could. This is a huge tragedy—and Colleen is just the best person in the world and doesn't deserve this. I mean, Ally didn't either. She was cold as ice, but I'm still sorry as all hell. But seriously—this has to be something local, right? Or some cult out of New Orleans. I heard they had a similar murder—it's on the news. People killed in a private family cemetery."

"Yes, people were killed in New Orleans," Danni said.

"Crazy people everywhere, right? Sick! The newscaster was talking about a possible cult sacrificing to a harvest god or the like. They don't really harvest a lot in the French Quarter or in the City of New Orleans, do they?"

"No, they don't," Danni said.

"People—they're scary as hell, huh?" he said. "That's why I'm far more than what most people think—a bouncer of some kind. I look people up. I find out about them. I keep the pedophiles and pretenders off our site." He rose then, looking down at her. "I want to help. If I think of anything, anything at all, I'll make sure that I tell your Mr. Quinn."

"Thank you," Danni said, rising herself. She wanted to see how Colleen was doing and then get to her room and call Quinn. She also wanted to get back to the diaries and books no library should have really let her take out—but Perryville was small. Also didn't hurt to befriend the librarian.

It might be important to tell Quinn about Yvette's diary and about the relationships—and lack of them—that had taken place between Ally Caldwell and her co-workers.

***

"On both Miss Caldwell and our John Doe," Dr. Harper said, "I believe the killer to have been right-handed. He came upon his victims from behind, grabbed them, and slit their throats hard and fast, causing death almost instantly with that kind of blood spill. We're working on it, but we don't know the name of our second victim."

Peter Ellsworth had reached the morgue ahead of Quinn and Larue.

Photographs had been taken; the bodies had been cleaned.

There was no small talk as they stood at the side of the body the doctor worked over—that of Allison Caldwell.

Ellsworth stepped back, not wanting his voice to ruin the integrity of the recording Dr. Harper had been making through the microphone that hung above the body.

He spoke softly, saying, "We've had a police artist do a sketch for us on our unknown male victim—we'll be getting the image out on the news, and hopefully someone will know who he is. We've asked for help from Lafayette, Baton Rouge, and New Orleans as well, so we don't believe it will be long."

Harper continued speaking.

"Miss Caldwell's cause of death was the initial strike, that which severed the jugular vein and all major vessels within the throat, causing quick exsanguination—the rest of the injuries were done post-mortem—twenty more stab wounds." He turned off the recording machine, looking from Larue to Ellsworth and then Quinn. "I believe the murders were made to appear even more brutal than they were," Dr. Harper said. "Death was fairly quick—both victims would have lost consciousness quickly and died almost immediately after. The stab wounds were for show."

Quinn looked at Larue. "What about the victims in NOLA?" Quinn asked.

"The same; Hubert is on the case," Larue said.

Quinn liked Dr. Hubert—they'd wound up working a very strange case that had involved one of his ancestors together. He had come to know the man and appreciate his talent and his integrity.

"When were they killed?" Quinn asked. If Harper believed it had been before midnight or one A.M., he could eliminate many people—those who had been at the mixer.

"We found our New Orleans victims yesterday, early morning as well—but they'd been there for hours before they were discovered," Larue said.

"Plenty of time for a killer to drive out here," Quinn murmured.

"Oh, yes, definitely. Your victims were killed a day before the victims here," Dr. Harper said. "My best estimation on Miss Caldwell and our John Doe is that they were killed sometime soon after midnight—probably five or six hours before they were discovered. I investigate the bodies and you investigate the rest, but I'm thinking my estimate of sometime between midnight and one is just about on the money, though there are, of course, variables that make any estimation just that—an estimate of time."

"But no earlier?" Quinn asked.

Harper shook his head. "No. After midnight. Both victims were facing away from the killer. They were taken by complete surprise. There are no defensive wounds. The killer slipped up behind each of them and struck with speed and strength. A right-handed killer, making the slash deep and hard, from the left to the right."

"Same as in New Orleans," Larue murmured.

"Same everything?" Quinn asked, looking from Harper to Larue.

Dr. Harper answered that. "I wasn't in New Orleans, but Detective Larue has had Dr. Hubert and I exchange photos and information from our crime scenes. It does appear that the 'scarecrows' were set up the same, and that the killings themselves were the same. Oh—there are fewer bones in the New Orleans picture, but in a private cemetery, you're not going to have as many dead to draw upon."

"No," Quinn said, glancing at Larue. He'd known Larue had been communicating with his team back in New Orleans and with the morgue. He'd done some of his calling from the car, but they'd reached the morgue too quickly for him to know everything that had been said. "Why would the killer have picked that cemetery when he had St. Louis I, II, and III to choose from in the city and massive cemeteries in Metairie?"

Larue shook his head.

"Line of sight," Ellsworth suggested. "Out here, who the hell was going to see what was going on—unless some teenagers were out to get high or fool around? Same thing—maybe the killer knew only one person lived in the old mansion, and they didn't have video security. Maybe, had the young woman who owned the place happened upon the killer, she would have just wound up as a victim on a scarecrow, too."

"Don't mind me—though you are at my autopsy," Dr. Harper said. "Calculating and running theories is good—so you should get to it. You can stay for the bitter details, but I'll give you full reports as soon as I've completed the autopsies."

"I think you're right. I think our time might be better spent trying to figure out how these people came to be this way—and not if, but where, the killer intends to strike again," Quinn said, "and Larue, we do need to know everything we can about the

New Orleans victims. Find out if there is any relationship between them and our victims here."

"You don't think this is simply a sick mind at work? They were taken by random selection—say, Miss Caldwell simply being in the wrong place at the wrong time? What association might she have with a young tourist in New Orleans? She was from New York, wasn't she?"

"Yes, she was from New York," Quinn said. "But Colleen Rankin also has a small office in New Orleans. There could be a connection. Or it could be a play upon old legends or superstitions."

"I'm going back to the Honeywell Lodge," Peter Ellsworth said. "I left officers out there while we were at the cemetery, but I'd like a chance to do a little milling and questioning myself. What is your plan, Larue—Quinn?"

Quinn glanced at his watch. It was getting late—six. Dark out already. He wanted to get to New Orleans, but two hours in and two hours out—maybe a little less, maybe a little more.

"We can head out for the city early tomorrow," Larue said.

Quinn nodded. He wanted to go that night. At the same time, he didn't feel comfortable about leaving Danni there at night. He could ask her to come with him, but he had a feeling Danni was more useful here. She had an easy personality and usually managed a quick rapport with people—especially when they looked on a private eye or a cop with wariness and suspicion.

"We'll head out first thing in the morning. Tonight, I want to see if I can hunt down any connection between the victims and continue the hunt for the car."

"All of our officers are aware they need to be on the lookout for an abandoned car, a dark sedan," Ellsworth said. "We know that because we have a witness as to the fact it was here—a man who saw the car."

"What?" Quinn said.

"John Appleby. Looks like a skeleton of an old rock star, but he's really an intelligent, decent and hardworking man. He happened by the cemetery and saw Ally Caldwell. It was late; he had been returning from one of his meetings and saw Ally outside the cemetery. He stopped and offered her a ride. She ran into the cemetery. Said he said he saw the car—a dark sedan, black, he thinks, and he saw Ally Caldwell. He was the last one to see her alive."

"What time?"

"Somewhere around midnight, he thinks," Ellsworth said.

"Is it possible to see him and speak with him?" Quinn asked.

"Sure. He'll meet us at the lodge, if you wish—and if we buy him some dinner. That always helps," Ellsworth said.

"I'd love to buy him some dinner," Quinn said.

"Let's do it then, shall we?" Larue suggested. "It's late and getting later."

Dr. Harper cleared his throat. "I will let you all have the reports as soon as possible. By the way, we may not have identified our male victim yet, but we have identified our corpse. The gentleman turned to straw with the others was Creighton Leary, interred last week in the cemetery in his family vault."

Peter Ellsworth stated at him. "You're just telling me that?"

Dr. Harper tapped the earpiece he was wearing. "Just got a positive I.D. in."

"Then we need to get back to the cemetery—get our crime scene investigators all over the Leary tomb!" Ellsworth said.

"You should do that, of course, but you're not going to find anything," Quinn said.

Ellsworth stared at him indignantly.

"Every murderer makes a mistake somewhere," he said.

"Yes, true—possible. Crime scene investigators need to be out there. But I'm heading back to the lodge, see what I can find out from people—and the Internet," Quinn told him. "I suggest, too, you get your people looking into every cemetery in the area. I'm afraid this killer might well strike again tonight, if not tonight, then very soon."

"He might strike in Baton Rouge, or Lafayette, New Iberia—St. Charles!" Ellsworth said.

"I think it's going to be here," Quinn said.

"Why is that? What evidence?" Ellsworth asked.

"No evidence. But this guy likes threes. Three scarecrows. And two scenes, so far. That means a third display is in the offing. Do I have evidence? No. This is sheer gut feeling, but I want to get to the lodge. I want to get on the computer, and I want to talk to your eye witness, Mr. John Appleby. He just may know more than he knows he knows!"

Chapter 6

"What will I do without her?" Colleen asked Danni. "Ally...people thought she was cold, but I think she had a rough childhood. Her dad wanted her to be a boy, and honestly, I think she just spent her life trying to prove herself. I just can't believe she's dead...oh, and I'm so sorry about that other man. What if it's all my fault. If I hadn't found this place, we wouldn't have been out here. I mean, it had to have been...a local thing, right? Well, NOLA and here...a Louisiana thing. I'm from this state and I love it, but I brought her here, and now..."

"Colleen, please!" Danni begged her. "You can't take the blame, and we don't know what happened yet, but it is not your fault at all. Please, please, please! Bad things happen," Danni said, hugging her friend.

They were alone in Colleen's suite—a beautiful room with a whirlpool tub, a balcony that looked over beautiful countryside, and a large, plush bed. It was a great room—but Danni thought Colleen needed to be out of it. She had been sitting in here—crying—when Danni had come up to see how she was doing.

She was glad she had done so. Colleen was not doing well.

"Someone might have wanted Ally, specifically, dead, Colleen, and no matter where you were, if she was or wasn't with you, they might have come for her."

Colleen stared at her as if she'd completely lost her mind.

"Someone after Ally? So, they killed two people in NOLA, another man here—and dug up two corpses?" she asked incredulously.

"Anything is possible," Danni told her. Her voice sounded weak in her own ears.

Colleen shook her head. "Why would anyone want Ally dead?"

That was an interesting question, but Danni thought she shouldn't try to explain what she'd learned. While Colleen might have seen the good in Ally, others had seen a cold and grasping woman who just might step on anyone to reach her own goals.

But even so—what would that have to do with similar murders in New Orleans?

"You have to get out of this room, Colleen. You need to be with friends. I know Tracy Willard was very concerned about you. Larry is upset, too. You have many people here who adore you—they love what you've done for them."

Colleen nodded bleakly. "Yes, I believe in people, and I believe in love, but..."

"Did Tracy find you?"

Colleen nodded again. "I—I told her I was fine. I asked her to see to the guests." She shook her head again. "I try to do good things—and they turn out like this!"

"Your heart is beautiful, and you do good things. You have to keep doing good things—because that helps balance out the bad in the world," Danni told her. "Colleen, you have to be strong—people will be looking to you for help and guidance."

"I should cancel everything," she said. "No, I can't. For some people, this has been a big splurge. I mean, we're very reasonable in what we charge, but people may get one vacation a year...time off from work, transportation...oh, I don't know! What would be right? What would be wrong?"

As if in answer to her questions, there was a knock at the door. Danni leapt up and hurried to open it.

Tracy was there. She looked at Danni hopefully, as if anxious to see if Danni had managed to make Colleen feel any better.

"Tracy, come on in!" Danni said.

Tracy did so and said, "What I really want to do is get Colleen to come with me—some of us from the main office want to get together—have our own little memorial. We'll talk about Ally, the good and the bad, and decide what to do."

"That's a great idea. You need to be with people, Colleen," Danni said.

For a moment, she wasn't sure how Colleen was going to react, but suddenly she stood—as if resolute.

"Yes! We will talk about Ally; we will remember her," she said.

"You're welcome to join us," Tracy told Danni.

Danni thought about the diaries and books in her room—about the fact she still hadn't had a conversation with Quinn, but being with this group just might give her something that couldn't be gotten anywhere else.

Except, Colleen was right. It was hard to figure how a determination to kill one woman could connect with murders back in New Orleans.

There was still so little they knew!

"Of course. I didn't know Ally, but—"

"We could use you!" Tracy said.

"Okay," Danni agreed. "Let's go. Wait, where are we going?"

"The restaurant has set us up at a back table," Tracy said. She hesitated. "After...Colleen, one of us needs to make a little speech to the guests."

"I will make the speech; it's my responsibility," Colleen said. She forced a smile through her tears and walked out the door leaving Danni and Tracy to follow.

***

"She took one look at me and decided I was trash," John Appleby said, shaking his head and looking from Peter Ellsworth to Larue and on to Quinn. "I just wanted to help. I could see she was standing there, and I couldn't see anything in the damned cemetery. If some jerk was playing a trick on her and disappearing, I was more than happy to get her where she needed to be. Lord, Peter," he said, addressing the parish cop, "you know me! I guess I'm not so pretty, but then again...I'm trying to feel bad about what happened, but she looked at me like pure trash. Can't say she was a sweetie or anything like that. Not that anyone should be murdered!" he added.

"Did you see anything in the cemetery at all?" Larue asked.

Appleby shook his head. "It was dark. I kind of figured if the fool woman wanted to run into the cemetery to find her driver or whatever, let her do it. I mean, usually...well, you know, the folks you find in a cemetery don't usually do you much harm, right?"

"No, not usually," Quinn murmured.

They'd met up with Appleby in the large circular drive in front of the grand entry for the hotel. The place had been built to resemble a beautiful Victorian façade with the driveway being especially large and inviting, arcing around a circular garden area with benches and little statues.

Appleby sat on a bench—not intimidated by the two cops and Quinn who stood and listened to his story.

Quinn was glad; he didn't want anyone else hearing the man. It might not pay to have someone think there had been a witness—even a witness who hadn't seen anything except for Ally running into the cemetery.

"What about the car you saw?" Quinn asked. "Do you remember anything about it?"

"Oh, yeah, it was a black sedan. Nice car, and up to date. One of those vehicles car services use, clean, spiffy, all that. Seen a bunch of them in the last few days—bringing in Miss Rankin, her staff and guests, too. To get here, you know, you're going to land in Baton Rouge or New Orleans, maybe even Lafayette, but you're still going to have to take a car to get to the Honeywell Lodge."

"Right, of course," Quinn said.

"Anything else at all?" Larue asked hopefully.

"Really, anything at all, about Miss Cantrell or the car. Anything," Quinn said.

The old man thought for a minute and suddenly brightened. "Masks!" he exclaimed suddenly.

"Masks?" Quinn asked.

John Appleby nodded, happy to have something to say. "You know, hanging from the rearview mirror—like some people have dice. Fuzzy dice or other stuff...this car had little Mardi-Gras masks, a pair of them, hanging from around the mirror. They were purple and gold. Half-masks. I remember seeing them when I drove on and glanced in the car."

A license plate or even a few letters or numbers from the plate would have been nice.

But he'd given them something.

"I wish I had more—I just don't," Appleby said. "I was...well, dang it, I was pissed—can't help it. A man doesn't like to be looked at like trash, you know? I just happened to see the masks. If I'd any idea people were going to wind up dead, I'd have read the damned license plate. I just happened to notice the masks."

"Thank you, Mr. Appleby. Your words may help a great deal," Quinn said.

"Can I go now? The dinner invite was great, but I've got the grandkids coming by today, and you know, my place is on the other side of all the land owned by Trent Anderson—thankfully. I'm not a-scared of cemeteries, but right now, with the kids coming...I'm just glad there's a little distance between us."

"Yes, of course, Mr. Appleby, thank you so much for coming to talk to us—deeply appreciated," Quinn said, and Larue and Ellsworth echoed his words.

Appleby nodded his thanks to them, stood, and surveyed the three of them. "You know where to find me if you need me. And you know about this area...legends and all. The witch who killed her husband and servant and then mysteriously wound up dead herself—three on scarecrows, just like this. Yep. Three on scarecrows. Someone brought it all the way to New Orleans. How do you like that? Our legend in the big city."

He paused suddenly, frowning. Then he shook his head.

"What is it?" Quinn asked.

"Nothing."

"What?" Peter Ellsworth asked anxiously. "John, if you have something..."

"I wish I had something. I was just thinking. There was something hanging with the masks...something like strung on the mirror, too. But tiny—like someone's necklace or a medallion or something like that. But...I may not even have seen it. I was just trying to picture in my mind's eye when I drove by...thought something glittered in my headlights. I could be wrong. I don't know what it might have been. Probably doesn't really matter. The car's gone, right? And the driver? Though the driver is probably the guy who died with Miss Ally. Anyway, don't know more, but I intend to be careful. You gentlemen watch yourselves, too, you hear?"

"We will do so," Peter Ellsworth promised him gravely.

John Appleby headed over to the circular drive and his truck.

They watched as he walked away with a surprisingly swift and agile walk.

"I'm heading up to my room. I want to check in with my people back in NOLA," Larue said. "Colleen told me this morning just to check at the desk. She'd see there were keys left for me."

"Call me," Quinn told him.

"And me," Ellsworth said. He looked at Quinn. "We need to spread out. I'm going to check the registry here—Find out who has been here too long to have murdered anyone two nights ago in New Orleans. Although," he said, and paused shaking his head. "It's a two-hour drive. Just a two-hour drive. If it was in the middle of the night..."

"Yeah," Quinn said. "Still, can't hurt to know. If we could find the car John Appleby saw, that might help a hell of a lot, too."

"Officers from both parishes are on it," Ellsworth assured him.

"I'm going to find Danni and see what she's discovered. You never know what information might have something that has to do with...something we've learned."

Ellsworth looked at him bleakly. "Only we haven't really learned anything," he said.

Quinn sighed, lowering his head, raising it again—surprised Ellsworth needed a pep talk.

"We've learned the identity of the corpse that was dug up. We know the killer started in New Orleans and brought his lethal appetites out here. We know there are all kinds of legends that go with that cemetery—and usually, there's a grain of truth that goes with legends. Which doesn't mean the killer is a wiccan or a voodoo priestess or any other such thing, it might just mean the killer knows the legends and wants us to believe what's happening now has to do with the past, with ghosts or goblins or something evil. Now, we need to narrow down suspects, and determine if it is something local—perpetrated by a person or persons—who knew the legend, or just someone who found out bits and pieces about the legend and decided it would be a nicely confusing way to commit murder."

"But a girl and a drunk in New Orleans. Then Ally Caldwell and a John Doe here—and a corpse. I can't even figure a direction to go in that makes real sense."

"You'll need to find out what you can about the local population. I'd say Trent Anderson could use some scrutiny," Quinn told him.

Peter Ellsworth nodded and turned back for his car. He lifted a hand in the air. "You start here. I'll be back. I will pay a visit to Mr. Anderson. After all, he is a next-door neighbor to the old harvest of the dead!"

Quinn wanted to talk to Trent Anderson himself, but first, Danni and a few of Colleen Rankin's employees. He headed in, dialing Danni's number as he did so.

He thought he heard her phone ringing in response to his call.

He did.

Looking past the coffee shop to the more elegant restaurant, he saw she was at a circular back table.

She was with Tracy Willard, Larry Blythe, Albert Bennett, and Colleen Rankin.

Colleen's face remained flushed and tear-stained, but she looked better than she had. It had only been that morning she'd discovered one of her most prized employees and presumed friend was dead—brutally murdered.

Danni hadn't seen him, and she was excusing herself to answer her phone, standing and stepping a few feet from the table.

"Hi," Quinn said.

"Hi—a long time since I've heard from you!" she said. "Are you...coming back here soon?"

"Very soon—" he told her, "I'm looking right at you,"

She frowned and looked up. By that time, he'd reached the restaurant entrance. She strode toward him, speaking softly and quickly, "Quinn, I found some incredible treasures at the library—not sure they'll help us any, but I have a diary by a young woman named Yvette, and I think she might *the* Yvette who brought about the legend. The librarian was wonderful. Quinn, I have research material no other library in the country would have let out of their sight. Which may not help. Anything—do you have anything at all?"

"Slow down. We'll talk. Should we join your party? Have you learned anything from them?"

"I can tell you all about it when we're alone," Danni said.

"Let's make that soon. I need to get on the computer." He was quiet a minute. "Maybe we'll go for a drive."

"A drive?"

"I want to find that car. Check out any other cemeteries."

"Maybe the fairgrounds," Danni said."

"Fairgrounds," he murmured.

"The Harvest Festival Fairgrounds," Danni said. "Jeanine—our lovely waitress—has been telling us all about the fair. It's a huge deal around here."

"Right. I heard that. And yes, we need to check out the fairgrounds. Beyond a doubt. But it's Wednesday night, how late could a fair here be open?"

"Late enough. They've taken a bit of a cue from New Orleans. Monday through Friday, they're open until midnight—and give guests another hour to make their way out. Saturday and Sunday night, they stay open to two or half past, giving guests, again, another hour to get out."

"So, they're wild and woolly out here."

"That from a man who lives a block off Bourbon Street?"

"Hey, Royal is quiet and refined. We're the restaurant-slash-museum-art shop and antiques street of the Quarter, remember?" he said lightly.

"Don't forget, Colleen's harvest ball is Saturday night. It has me uneasy. Everything has me uneasy. I'm worried about other cemeteries, the fairgrounds—and this lodge," she said softly.

"Danni," he said softly, "your friends are looking at us."

"Well, they know you're a P.I. involved with the cops," she reminded him. "Don't play around it; answer what questions you can."

Albert Bennett and Larry Blythe rose politely as they neared the table. Danni took her seat; Quinn paused to give Colleen a hug. He didn't ask how she was doing. He took a seat at the table.

Naturally, everyone was staring at him.

"Anything?" Tracy asked anxiously.

"Our investigation has just begun," Quinn said gently.

Tracy sat back, disappointed. "The news seems to have more info than the police," she said. "Everyone knows a tourist was found dead like Ally in New Orleans—with another guy and then an already-dead guy. Weird. Of course, you didn't discover anything—this has to be the work of a cult—crazy people who think they're reborn witches. Some awful group determined to bring out pagan rituals or something like that. Such a shame Ally got caught in it!"

"Yes sad. It's sad when anyone is so brutally murdered," Quinn said, "and you can't bring anyone back, but you can find justice for them."

Tracy sighed. "I hope so!" she said fervently. "But...well, this person could be done and gone and...well, they never caught Jack the Ripper or the Zodiac or dozens more. That could be the case here."

Colleen let out a little sniffle.

"We won't let that be the case here!" Danni said passionately. The group turned to look at her and she blushed lightly. "I, uh, know Detective Larue out of New Orleans, and he—and Quinn—will not let that happen."

"Do you think the killer has already moved on?" Larry asked anxiously, pushing his glasses back up his nose.

"Never count on a killer having moved on. People need to stay safe—and watch out for strangers," Albert Bennett said. He frowned then. "Quinn, you've been out on this all day. Can we get you something to eat?"

"No, no, I'm good, thank you!" Quinn said. He wasn't—he was starving. But he knew the hotel had room service, and he wanted to get to the room. "I would really like a shower, so I think I'm going to head on up."

"Of course!" Tracy said. "You've been dealing with corpses."

Colleen let out another sniffle.

"Oh, God, I'm so sorry!" Tracy said.

Colleen shook her head. "No, no, I'm all right. I've sent out an email to all of our guests, telling them I'd like a word with everyone—or anyone who can make it—in the lobby at 8:30. It's just about time."

"You sent out an email?" Albert said, surprised.

Colleen nodded firmly. "Yes. I'm going to be strong. I need to tell everyone they're free to leave with no penalty if they wish. I'm going to say we're in mourning—we have lost a beloved colleague, but we know how much this event means to people, and we will be going on as intended."

"Bravo, Colleen," Albert murmured.

"I think that...I think we can't just fold up with so many people here, and you are entirely right," Tracy said.

"I guess," Larry murmured.

"Everyone was here for the opening event last night, right?" Quinn asked lightly.

"I know you know I was here. I spoke with you," Albert Bennett said.

"Me, too," Tracy murmured.

"That's right. I saw when Danni introduced you to Quinn," Albert said. "You may not remember, because you were ogling that millionaire."

"Albert, I was...welcoming an important guest!" Tracy said.

"We're supposed to be making connections for others here," Larry said, looking at Tracy.

"We make the right connections with the right people," Tracy said, glaring at the other two.

Colleen didn't even seem to hear them. She glanced at her watch. "Just a few minutes now."

"Yes, of course, Trent Anderson was here, too," Quinn said, his smile totally innocent as he looked at Tracy.

Tracy stood up, quickly talking to Colleen. "If you're making an announcement in just a few minutes, we should get out to the lobby."

"Yes, excuse me," Colleen said.

"We'll all go," Quinn said. "I, uh, do we need to get a check?"

"They know I'll take care of them," Colleen said, and she smiled at him, as if very grateful he was there. He gave her a nod of encouragement, and her head seemed to hike up just a bit.

Danni slipped her arm through Colleen's.

"Ready?"

They led the way out. In the lobby many of the guests were milling already—talking amongst themselves. They all stared at Colleen, some giving her pitying glances and a few looking wary as if they dreaded what her words might be.

"There's a steady chair there Colleen can stand on," Quinn said quietly to Danni. "I'm going to get it. It will let her tower a bit above the crowd."

A minute later they had Colleen standing high on the chair; no one had to ask for silence, the room went silent. You could have heard a pin drop.

"My friends," Colleen said. "I thanked you the other night for coming—for helping me realize my dream of a place not just to interact on the Internet, but in person. A gathering of those who want to know the possibilities in flesh and blood—rather than just through pictures and words. A place where, when you have met, you can come...and have fun with others or alone. But I'm sure you've all heard by now that there is a killer out there, possibly a serial killer. He struck in New Orleans and here...and here, he struck one of our own, our beloved Allison Caldwell. We are, of course, devastated. But Ally believed in what we were doing, too. She was key in opening this lodge, in making all of the arrangements. What has happened is horrible beyond imagination, and if you wish to cut short your time here, there will be no penalties. If you wish to stay, we will be here, and the Harvest Fest Ball will go on as planned; the lodge will remain open." She glanced down at Quinn. "I'm encouraged to have Mr. Quinn here—along with my old and dear friend, Danni Cafferty. They might be talking to you—along with the police, they will find out what happened to Ally. And they will do their best to see that no one else suffers her fate."

Applause greeted her words.

"Quinn," Colleen murmured, stooping down to him. "Tell them to be safe!"

He nodded, glad he was tall enough to tower above most of the crowd without having to step up on the chair. He raised a hand to show he was going to speak.

"The important thing here is to be safe—don't go off on your own. This killer has murdered both men and women. Don't go anywhere alone. Don't wander in the dark. Lock your doors, keep with a crowd as much as you can."

"Orgy!" Someone called, bringing about a spurt of uneasy laughter.

"Only if you know everyone in your group," he said lightly, not wanting to come with so heavy a hand they didn't listen. "Seriously, please, be smart. Be careful. That includes wandering in any dark areas alone, or even in isolated areas alone by the light of day. We aren't sure how and when all the victims were taken."

"Were they killed in the middle of our opening?" a man called to him. "Wouldn't that mean all of us are...more or less safe?"

He decided to tell the truth. "No, the victims were killed just after midnight, so the medical examiner believes. So please, be smart, be careful. That's all."

"Wait!" someone else called out. "What about New Orleans—did this guy follow us out here?"

"We just don't know any more yet," Quinn said. "Please, watch yourselves. And excuse me now."

He grabbed Danni's hand and headed for the elevators. Questions followed him, and he answered all with, "We just don't know any more, yet."

He managed to get into the elevator with Danni—followed by a group of people who slipped in still asking questions.

"I heard there's a bunch of legends about that cemetery," an anxious girl, tiny and worried, noted staring at Quinn.

"Cursed Yvette! She's come back to kill people," a young blond added solemnly.

"Well, we can stay the hell out of the cemetery," A dark-haired man said.

"And anywhere remote!" Danni added, "Even as couples. Beautiful rooms here—keep the, um, intimate meetings behind locked doors."

They stepped off on their floor.

One man—the dark-haired fellow who had spoken in the elevator—followed them off.

Quinn sighed, holding Danni's hand. "It's been a long day for us—"

"I'm Joshua Grayson. I was with my match, Zoey Nixon, in the cemetery. We were the ones to first discover the bodies," he said.

Chapter 7

Danni wasn't sure what the man could add to what they knew, but Quinn invited him into their room.

Colleen had been good to them. Their room was very much like the suite she had taken for herself.

There was a whirlpool tub with a charming tapestry-like curtain that could be drawn to separate the tub from the rest of the room.

They had a balcony that looked over the outdoor pool. There was a sitting area with a loveseat and a chair, and it was there Joshua Grayson spoke, telling him how he and Zoey had a love of history—something that had brought them together online before they'd met in person—and they'd heard of the historic cemetery and had longed to explore it.

"We didn't see the scarecrows—the bodies—when we first got there. Some of the oldest in-ground graves and some amazing funerary art are there, right beyond the arched gates. We were truly enjoying the history—and," he added dryly, "finding four stones and a tomb with the name 'Yvette' on it, before we were in far enough to see the scarecrows and then...we didn't think that they were anything at first. Just scarecrows—apparently, there's an old superstition, going way back to Europe, that three scarecrows will keep demon spirits away. Or something like that. I've heard the legend with a few variations, but...it didn't seem so strange to see scarecrows. Then," he paused, inhaling and exhaling, "and then, we realized they weren't just straw, they were human beings dressed up in straw, and...we freaked. Zoey thought to call 911—while we were running out. The police asked us to stay—I told them I was terrified to do so, but I guess a dispatcher called Detective Ellsworth right away, and he was there within a few minutes. He thought we were crazy at first—or pulling a sick joke. There was already news out about bodies having been found in New Orleans the morning before. He asked us to go back into the cemetery with him. It was...horrible."

"Did you see anyone else while you were there?" Quinn asked him.

"I didn't, and I don't know if it was because she was afraid or not, but Zoey said she was certain someone had been watching us from one of the mausoleums or crypts or whatever you call the little family mausoleums."

"But you saw no one?" Danni asked softly.

He shook his head. "No one."

"What about a car?" Quinn asked. "And just what time was it when you were there?"

"My car was the only one I saw. We parked right outside of the gates."

"And the time?" Danni persisted.

"Right after an early breakfast; we, uh, both woke early. Had breakfast in bed. We'd planned on taking part in the trivia contest yesterday around lunchtime, so we wanted to get there. I'm thinking we got to the cemetery right about eight-thirty."

"Did you see or hear anything else at all?" Quinn asked hopefully.

Joshua shook his head. "But I wanted to make sure to talk to you. I wanted you to know it was Zoey and me who were there first." He hesitated. "Zoey is from Baton Rouge. She said she was so close to this place, and she'd never been in the cemetery. Said she knew a lot about legends that had to do with the area. The woman—Yvette—supposedly murdered by her would-be mother-in-law just to take revenge and rise from the grave to kill her a year later. And the scarecrows. Three. There must always be three." He hesitated. "I guess I really...hate to say it, but I'm scared. Zoey and I discovered the dead. And three...yes, there were three scarecrows there already. But three were killed in New Orleans. I'm afraid the killer is planning on another three—and neither Zoey nor I want to be part of that three." He looked from Quinn to Danni anxiously. "I, uh, wonder if we need some kind of special protection."

"I'm not a policeman, you know," Quinn reminded him, "but I can talk to Detective Ellsworth." He hesitated. "Even considering a homicide goes to the parish police, we're talking a small area out here and small police forces. Maybe I can ask he put a man on detail out here."

"I'd be willing to pay you to be a personal bodyguard. I'm not Trent Anderson rich, but I do well enough to pay you. I don't want to leave, and I don't want Zoey to leave. This guy hit New Orleans and here—he could be aiming for Baton Rouge next. Or he could just stay here and kill again."

Quinn nodded somberly at the man's reasoning. "I can't be your bodyguard; I have committed to helping investigate what's going on. But I'll see what I can do. For tonight, go to your room. Lock in. When you're out, stay with the crowd."

"We'll stay in the lodge," Joshua promised, rising. "Trust me, we'll stay here. And anything you can do...deeply appreciated."

They all stood. Quinn walked him to the door. Joshua looked uneasily up and down the hallway.

"You know, there are security cameras in the hallways and elevators," Quinn said.

"Yeah—the cops will be able to watch my murder. That will be great," Joshua said.

Quinn turned to Danni. "Lock in—I'll get Mr. Grayson back to his room. What about Zoey?"

"Zoey is there—she hasn't come out since we returned from the cemetery."

"I'm fine—go," Danni told Quinn.

He met her eyes; she was determined.

He knew better than to fight with her.

"Lock the door?"

"You bet!" she assured him. He heard the door close, then the bolt slide.

"Come on, Mr. Grayson—I'll get you back to your room. And Zoey."

He started down the hall with Joshua Grayson. They saw no one on their way to the elevator, no one in the elevator, and no one in the hallway when they got off at the next floor.

Joshua called out at the door to assure Zoey it was him. A timid young woman with soft brown hair in a ponytail opened the door and looked at Quinn with wide eyes.

"My escort," Joshua said, grinning ruefully, "but he won't work for us."

Zoey's face seemed to turn white.

"As I said, I will check into what the police might be able to do," Quinn said.

"Three! This whole thing is about three!" Zoey said. "There's going to be another three."

Quinn had the same fear himself, but he didn't want to add to her paranoia. He believed that, locked in their room, here at the lodge, they would be fine.

"You two are both history buffs, right? I hear about two legends—the witch who killed her handyman and her husband and the three scarecrows, and the legend that revolves around Yvette."

"Yes, there are two legends," Zoey said.

"Can you figure anyway they might twist together?" Quinn asked her.

Zoey stared at Joshua. "I...I don't know. I believe the Yvette story is a real one—though, if it was her lover's mom or not, I don't know. I guess it was blamed on her—and she wound up dead a year later. Strange thing is they are supposedly buried—rather interred—together."

"Really? Where?"

"I'm not sure—that was something we were going to try to find out about. I mean, Yvette became a legend. The legend doesn't give her a last name." She hesitated a minute. "From what I understand though, she was murdered at harvest time."

"Thank you," Quinn said, "and I asked Joshua—can you think of anything you might have seen at the cemetery, seen or heard, you might have been too flustered to remember earlier?"

Zoey started to shake her head; her ponytail bobbed. Then she frowned and glanced at Joshua. "I—I thought we were being watched. From deep in the cemetery. I didn't want to wait for Detective Ellsworth to get there. I just wanted to get far, far away. It seemed like the trees were...moving. Far back. Beyond the mounds of hill tombs or whatever they are. I haven't seen anything like them in another Louisiana cemetery. I just felt I was being...watched. It scared me, but we stayed in the car—all locked up—and waited for Detective Ellsworth." She took a breath. "While we were in the car, we heard the news about New Orleans. I just want to get away—I want to go home, except home is far too close to this place!"

Quinn thanked her again and started down the hall.

"Mr. Quinn!" Zoey called.

He stopped and turned back.

"Three—I'm not sure what the legend of Yvette has to do with the number three, but...I'm really afraid. Three...would mean three threes!"

"Thank you," he said.

As he headed back for the elevator, he was afraid he very much so agreed with her.

The question was, where would the killer strike again? And just what the hell was it he meant to convey with the complexity of his displays?

One thing was sure; the sites were scoped out; the murderer was planning carefully.

They might not have a clue...

But the killer already knew exactly where and when he'd strike again.

***

Danni sat at the pretty white French-provincial desk where she'd left the books and diaries she'd garnered from the library. She mentally thought of all she wanted to tell Quinn, idly flipping through one of the books.

She stopped, coming upon an image of an old painting.

It was of a very pretty, dark-haired girl. She had large brown eyes and sweeping thick lashes, a slender nose, gracefully arched brows, and a generous mouth. Her smile was charming. She stared out from the copy of the old painting as if she were in love with life itself, in love with the world.

Beneath the picture was a caption.

Yvette Benoit. The beautiful child of a French farmer and his wife, murdered.

Danni quickly flipped around looking for dates. Yes, it was the Yvette who had penned the diary she had read earlier.

She glanced at the book that held the image; it was an old history novel of the area, printed by a college press back in 1910. She glanced quickly at the old flap; the author had been an historian who had lived in nearby New Iberia.

She quickly glanced over the pages that preceded the picture.

While legend had it she'd been murdered by her prospective mother-in-law, the author believed she had been killed by a jealous would-be lover.

Someone furious she would find an English-American more to her liking than someone from her own cultural background.

Danni studied the image of Yvette again. The young woman had been dressed as if for a ball in a beautiful gown. The shoulders dipped down, framed by lace. The bodice appeared to be velvet, low cut—but not too low. She wore a medallion, a fleur-de-lis medallion, not at all unusual anywhere in Louisiana.

Danni jumped when she heard Quinn return, knocking on the door and identifying himself before coming in and locking the door again.

She looked at him.

"I have so much to tell you," she said.

She rushed into his arms. For a moment they just held one another.

"What about New Orleans? Maybe we can get someone working on it back there—Billie, Father Ryan, Natasha..."

"I'm going to take a run back to the city tomorrow," he told her. "For now, this is what I know. The bodies in New Orleans were found in almost the exact same state as those here. Larue texted me pictures of the crime scene. One man already dead and disinterred, and a local man murdered just as the young woman. The only difference was that there were not as many bones strewn around the 'scarecrows.' Here's the thing—someone had to know about that cemetery. Most people living there have at least heard of the mansion, but the tourist brochures don't necessarily talk about the family cemetery. So, someone knew about that cemetery—and this cemetery, and all the legends about scarecrows. Whoever it was, obviously they were in New Orleans and then here. That, to me, implies it does have to be someone who has something to do with Colleen's group."

Danni stared searchingly into his eyes. "Maybe—and maybe not. A lot of these people are from different states—and even from different cities in Louisiana. We're both from New Orleans, but we'd never been in the cemetery out here."

"Danni, I think it was carefully planned. But one of the CSI women told us a story about a talisman that makes people go crazy. That's why I told you to be on the lookout for a talisman of some kind. Something small, I think. But...I don't know. Maybe there's something—maybe there's nothing."

"Are you thinking about Colleen's guests or clients?"

He shook his head gravely. "No, but her employees would have been out here as the place was being built—and in NOLA, too."

Danni nodded. "Yes. But it was one of her employees who was killed—along with a John Doe. And the woman in New Orleans—not sure what a New Orleans tourist could have to do with any of this. Do you know anything about her?"

"Young woman, a tourist just going through New Orleans, or so the landlady at her bed and breakfast told Larue."

"What was her name?"

"Belinda Cardigan."

"I'm just wondering—" Danni began.

"So am I. Can you get into the files for the corporation?" Quinn asked her. "Not just the files about people who are here, but anyone who might have come out, who might have been on one of Colleen's dating sites?"

"Sure, so could you—all we have to do is ask Colleen," Danni said.

Quinn nodded grimly. "Maybe. Better that you ask. Ellsworth could probably get a search warrant, but that could take time. Call Colleen. Tell her you need access to everything. If the police were to ask—even if I were to ask—being Colleen, she'd be concerned about the privacy rights of her people—even if they are laying it all out on the Internet for everyone to see."

"You want me to call her now? It's late."

He cocked his head as he looked at her, giving her a pained grimace. "Yes, I know it's late—but I'd also like to head back out."

"Oh?"

"I want to see the harvest fair grounds."

Danni nodded. "Okay." She fumbled on the desk for her cell phone and called Colleen. As she expected, her friend gave her a clear go ahead.

"Of course, anything—anything at all I can do. If we catch the guy who did this to Ally...I'd like to slit his throat myself in turn!" she said. "I'll tell you how to key into our site and give you my password—that way it will just appear I've been in there. Though I don't know if that matters or not." She sounded so strong. Then it seemed there was a little catch in her voice again. "I don't know much about legal matters. Ally and Albert kept me safe and secure. I...uh, well, I still have Albert."

Quinn looked at Danni, arching a brow.

"Full access," she said. "I can go into the site while we head out to the fairgrounds."

He nodded. "Ready?"

"You're going to hold on that shower, I take it?"

He didn't reply; he just opened the door for her.

They headed quickly out. They could see the social areas—coffee shop, bar, and restaurant—were going strong.

No one wanted to be alone.

"What are you thinking?" Quinn asked her, opening the door to head out to their car.

"I'm thinking there may be a lot of hook-ups—maybe no more than one-night-stands—after today."

"Most probably, except..."

"Except?"

"Maybe not. How would you know you're not hooking up with a killer?" Quinn asked.

Danni shrugged and pulled out her phone, punching in the access to Colleen's dating site even as she slid into the passenger seat of the car.

They drove, and as they were nearing the fairgrounds, she had gone through hundreds of names when she found the one she was seeking.

She gasped and stared over at Quinn.

He didn't take his eyes off the road.

"You found her; you found Belinda Cardigan. She was a client, a prospective match on Colleen's dating site. The only thing we don't know now is...was she headed out here?"

"I can keep digging," Danni said.

She started to look back at her phone, but they had reached the fairgrounds. The parking field had begun to empty; it was easy for them to drive up, close to the front.

And there, right at the entry, high above the ground, were three scarecrows.

One, two, three...

All stuffed well with straw and sporting pumpkin-head, large jack-o-lanterns that seemed to grin down at people as they arrived, grins that seemed to offer nothing but malice...

And pure evil.

Chapter 8

Last minutes tickets to the festival were extremely reasonable, and Quinn decided they should go in and look around—before perhaps finding someone in management and suggesting that, under the circumstances, the scarecrows were in very bad taste.

The poles stood about twenty feet high; the feet of the scarecrows were at just about ten feet; the pumpkin heads were beyond eerie.

Once they were in, they paused, staring at the things for several minutes.

"You don't think a killer could get in here and pose bodies up there, do you?" Danni asked. "That's high, and they must have security here. You couldn't leave a place with booths and rides and all kinds of things without security—could you?"

"I don't think so," Quinn said, pocketing his wallet. "But...anyway, let's take a walk around. Then, I think we should talk to someone about this."

"You're not going to get them to take those scarecrows down," Danni said.

"Why not?"

"Do you think you could get people not to throw beads at Mardi Gras?"

"If there had been a slew of 'murder by beads,' maybe," Quinn answered.

"The scarecrows are eerie, I imagine, because around here, they're supposed to protect people. This fair has been up for a while, and I don't think it goes down until after Thanksgiving, around the beginning of Christmas season. So, those scarecrows have been there for a bit."

"I know. I understand the harvest tradition around here. It's just now...there are dead people. Murdered by someone with an agenda, and that agenda has to do with scarecrows."

"Okay...you can try. For now, let's walk!"

They did so; the fair was arranged as a large oval with animal displays—including pigs raised by teens, chickens, rabbits, and more—between food booths and rides.

They passed by the kids' section first. Cute. Little cars went around on a small track. There was a train designed to appear to be a much beloved literary "character," and there were little swings.

One booth sold jambalaya, boudin, and more. Another offered every kind of hot sauce known to man. Yet another specialized in shrimp and grits and also crawfish etouffee.

They walked past a wicked looking coaster, and then a "twister," and then something called the giant—a lift that carried fair-goers way up high and then slid them along a steep slope. Finally, they came upon the "Castle of Terror." The outside of the ride featured movie monsters including vampires, werewolves, mummies, and more.

"Let's take this one," he suggested.

Danni arched a brow, wrinkling her face. "Really?"

"I want to see what's in it."

"You really think someone involved with the fair might be in on these murders?" she asked.

He shook his head. "No, but I don't like the giant scarecrows at the front of the fair, and I really want to see what's in this ride."

"Okay," Danni said.

They joined the short line that remained at the late hour. The young man checking their entry bracelets gave them a wide smile.

"Watch out for that big guy of yours!" he teased Danni. He cast Quinn an amused grin. "The big ones may need a lot of cuddling to get through this kind of a fear factory!"

"I'll protect him for all I'm worth," Danni promised.

They stepped into their little car.

"You're going to protect me?" Quinn asked.

Danni laughed and set her arm around him.

"Well, semi-romantic," he said softly.

The ride jolted. They went by evil jack-in-the-boxes, a black-widow woman with a beating heart in her hand, and the usual number of monsters, all motion-activated to do something frightening as each car went by.

It was fairly ho-hum. The usual fair ride.

Until they were at the end. Then, to their right, holding signs that bid the rider good night—and good luck—were three scarecrows.

Once again, they had pumpkin heads with faces eerily carved.

"Not good," Quinn murmured. "Not good."

"It's a ride," Danni reminded him.

"A ride—a dark ride. People scream as they go through it. It's hardly Fort Knox. I can see a dozen ways someone could slip in here."

"Okay, well...we can try to do something," Danni said. "Or you could call Detective Ellsworth who probably has a lot more clout around here."

She was right; but he didn't like the fair. He didn't like the scarecrows.

As they left the ride, he remembered he hadn't eaten. The aroma of food from some of the booths was strong and he looked at Danni.

"Food," he said simply.

"That should be easy enough."

The girl at a booth advertising "amazing" jambalaya was about to close up, but she smiled as they approached.

"I'm sorry. Am I too late?" Quinn asked.

"No, you have about ten minutes left, and we're easy. I'd have given you fifteen!"

He asked for jambalaya and a soda, and she went to dish up his food, returning and still smiling as she took his money and delivered his order.

Then she glanced uneasily down the path toward the entrance. A quick look of unease, and then she was smiling again.

"Is anything wrong?" Danni asked her.

She shook her head. "No, no, I love working the fair. I'm in the community college, but I'm hoping to head to New Orleans and Loyola! They're great here—I've worked it since I was sixteen. Saved a lot."

"That's great," Danni said. She smiled, too, but she persisted. "You look nervous, though. I guess we're all nervous."

The girl nodded. "The murders in the cemetery." She hesitated, biting her lip. "I, uh, well, we stay through the last customer, till we're sure everyone is out. I was cleaning up a bit early. I..."

"What?" Quinn demanded.

"I don't know—I'm imagining things, I think. I thought I heard someone in the crowd talking about scarecrows and bodies and...*Cursed Yvette,* and I'm a little freaked out. This area can get really quiet, and..."

"Hey, finish cleaning up. We'll walk you out when you're ready," Quinn said.

She stared at them and Danni whacked his arm lightly. "Quinn, show her your I.D. How does she know we're safe?"

"Right!"

"An investigator out of New Orleans?" the girl murmured. "Oh. Oh! There were murders there, too. It's really scary. I hope this guy has moved on. Not that I wish a murderer on the rest of the state, but...around here, scarecrows are a big thing, and I know I'll never look at one the same again!"

"I was wondering if the management might be willing to take them down," Quinn said.

"Management?" she asked. "This place is owned by just one man. Oh, I'm sorry—he has people in charge each night to watch out for problems and the like—taking care of any safety issues. And there are police officers here all the time during opening hours, along with private security. But if you want those scarecrows down, there's just one person to talk to. He's richer than Midas—but approachable. Nice guy, really—perhaps because he's from here. Inherited money, but he's done well with it, and from what I've seen, he never forgets where he came from—right here!"

"You're talking about Trent Anderson?" Quinn asked.

She nodded gravely and then offered her hand. "Mr. Quinn, I'm Daphne Alain. And," she said, offering her hand to Danni.

"Danni, Danni Cafferty," she said.

The girl smiled warmly at her.

"By the way, that's such a pretty pendant you're wearing," Danni said.

Quinn hadn't noticed her jewelry; he looked at the pendent but couldn't really see it then. Daphne had clutched it in one hand as she beamed at Danni.

"Thank you! It is pretty—but I'm afraid you'll see tons just like it! The motif is very popular around here, a copy of an antique piece, I think. They sell pendants just like it or a lot like it at one of the booths right here. If you come back when the place is open, you can see them. The booth is just past the monster ride!"

"Nice," Danni said. "If we come back, I'll definitely go see them."

"If you're really worried about the scarecrows—they're creeping me out this year, too—you should talk to Mr. Trent," Daphne said. "He really is a nice man."

"I guess we will talk to Mr. Trent Anderson then," Quinn said, looking at Danni.

Danni nodded and turned to Daphne. "We'll be at that table there until you're ready. Then, we'll see you to your car."

"Thanks!" the girl said. "Oh, would you like something? On the house."

"Thank you, I ate earlier, but that was sweet. I'm fine. We'll be fine waiting for you."

"Thanks!"

They headed to one of the picnic tables set up for diners by the food booths.

"You don't mind, do you? This is probably silly, and we could be out of here," he said to Danni.

She gave him a look of reproach and indignation. "Of course not!"

"What was the bit about her necklace?" Quinn asked Danni.

"I know what it's copied from. It's exactly like a pendant in the picture of Yvette. The Yvette whose diary I read and who—I believe—is the murdered Yvette of legend."

"But, she said—"

"Yes, that it's a common piece, sold at the fairgrounds, and by a dozen different outlets around here. Probably elsewhere—it's a fleur-de-lis."

"But, each fleur-de-lis might be different. And if we are looking for something...ah, hell. There could be a real pendant, causing all kinds of mayhem, and hundreds—or thousands—of knock-offs!"

"There could be," Danni said, adding dryly, "we could try to buy them all and find out."

He grimaced. "I have a feeling we wouldn't buy the real one. If there is such a thing, someone else already has it."

"How is the jambalaya?"

"Surprisingly good—delicious, actually."

"Good to hear. Maybe I'll try it—if we come back." She was silent a minute and then added, "Maybe we won't have to come back. Trent Anderson does seem like a decent person."

"Um. Sure, he was decent enough...and," he added, "hot and heavy with Colleen's redhead," Quinn said.

"It looks like her co-workers—Albert Bennett and Larry Blythe—know she's seeing him, too. And not so happy—maybe even trying to get her in trouble with Colleen. Colleen is just too distracted to notice right now, but I think Albert and Larry are wrong. If her employee made a great match, Colleen would be delighted, thinking she created a love-match one way or the other."

Quinn nodded, and then frowned. People had walked by them—many people. All leaving the fairgrounds, since rides and booths had now closed for the night. Fewer and fewer people straggled by them.

It was just about midnight.

He had a mouthful of food when he first noticed the shadow. He froze, listening to Danni, but not really hearing her.

Then he stood.

Daphne's fears had not been unfounded. He could see someone had slipped behind the booth—there was easy entry from the back. She could have a hand clamped over her mouth and be dragged back—with no one the wiser.

"Quinn?" Danni said.

He bolted around behind the booth, just in time for someone to jerk on one of the canvas coverings, causing it to fall between them and around them. Cursing, Quinn lifted it off himself, shouting for Daphne.

She leapt over the counter, screeching.

He freed himself, searching in every direction for a runner. Whoever it had been had managed to disappear into the brush that lay behind the set-up of the fair on the field. He could give chase, but most probably to no avail.

Besides, Danni and Daphne were alone.

He came around; Daphne was in Danni's arms, shaking.

"I quit! I quit!" she said. "Right before you came...I saw the shadow. I was about to scream. The other vendors...no one was here. If you hadn't waited for me...it might have been nothing. It might have been...oh!"

Danni looked searchingly at Quinn. He discretely shook his head. "We need to report this to Ellsworth and Larue," he said. "I know it's late, but..."

Daphne winced, looking downward. "I saw the shadow!" she said weakly. "Someone was coming for me. I'm happy to talk to anyone you want!"

Quinn took out his phone; Danni still held a shaking Daphne.

He called Larue first; the man answered the phone with a gruff voice. Quinn had obviously awakened him. He quickly grew sharp and promised to call Ellsworth and meet them just outside the entry to the fair.

In another twenty minutes, both Larue and Ellsworth were there. Quinn explained his concern about the scarecrows, but also said he'd be happy to talk with Trent Anderson himself.

Ellsworth swore to follow Daphne home and see she was locked in.

"You know, it could have just been some jerk trying to pick you up," Ellsworth told Daphne. "The whole parish is going a little bit crazy. I think we're going to have to call in some help from the state. Everyone is afraid."

"State help wouldn't be a bad thing," Quinn said.

"It probably was just some jerk!" Daphne said. "But my booth...I can't wind up alone out here anymore. I...want to make sure I live to get to a four-year college!"

Eventually, everyone got into their cars—Ellsworth following Daphne.

Larue was in his own vehicle.

Quinn revved the engine to the car he and Danni shared. She yawned suddenly.

"It's past one," she told him.

"Yeah. Long day. Really, really, really long day."

"But a good one—at the end. You saved her life."

"Maybe. Maybe we just stopped an ass from trying too hard to pick her up," Quinn said.

Danni shook her head. "I don't think so. I think your instincts were right. I think you just put a crimp into the killer's plans—and there won't be a display of three dead scarecrow-people tomorrow morning."

***

It was nearly two when they finally returned to their room at the Honeywell Lodge.

Danni was bone tired and knew Quinn had to be bone tired, too, but once in their room, he set his weapon and holster on the side of the bed and stripped down before heading toward the shower, kicking off his shoes, jumping on one foot and then other as he stripped off his socks, and shedding his jacket and shirt on his way to the bathroom.

She heard the shower and hesitated.

It seemed eons ago they had laid by the pool, teasing one another about romance.

Long, long, day—as they had said. Still, she stripped quickly herself, heading into the bathroom and joining him in the shower, stepping in behind him and curling her arms around his chest before laying her head on his back.

He turned to her, pulling her close, their bodies flush against one another.

"Poster boy, eh?" he teased softly.

"Um," she murmured.

The water sluiced around them as he lifted her chin and kissed her long and deep. The heat of the water and the steam around them seemed beautifully mystical, and yet as his hands slid down her back, mystical became increasingly arousing.

Quinn fumbled for the faucet and turned off the spray and for a moment he paused, looking into her eyes. He smiled, and she felt the extent of his arousal against her.

She smiled slowly as well as he stepped out, drawing her with him, and groped for a towel, dropping the first, securing the second.

He wrapped it around her and they met in a fierce kiss once again, one that brought them half dried and half still damp through the steam that embraced the bathroom out to the bedroom area and onto the large bed that dominated the room.

She loved the way he looked at her, the way he touched her. His hands were large, his fingers long, and as they played over the length of her, she felt a gasp of pleasure escaping her. She grinned and touched him in return. Their mouths met again in a fury of a kiss before his lips travelled, and her fingers played over his shoulders as his touches and kisses travelled the length of her.

He was an incredible lover, knowing when to tease, when to move like wildfire, whisper just the right words...

Forge together as one, writhe, twist, thunder...then hold her when the world exploded into beautiful crystals, and it was time to drift back to reality.

She curled against his naked body, stroking the dampness of his chest, feeling his heart beat, feeling him breathe.

"Early morning," he murmured.

"Very romantic," she said, and he laughed softly. Then he grew serious, drawing her up to look at him and rising on an elbow.

"I want to get into and out of New Orleans and then see Trent Anderson as soon as I'm back." He hesitated, running his fingers through his dark hair. "Do you want to come with me? It might be best."

She shook her head. "Oh, it's not that I don't want to come with you. I just think I'm better off staying here."

"Don't go—"

"'Walking into any spooky old woods alone?'" she said with a wry smile. "Trust me—I won't. But I do think I should be here. With Colleen—and just listening and gathering whatever it is we might get. I've barely touched the books and the diaries, and there might be something in them."

He nodded. "Okay." He touched her hair gently and drew his fingers down her face. "I guess our being back on this so quickly..."

"Sex...business...it's the way it goes."

He frowned as if pained and she quickly added, "Quinn, it's not like we have normal jobs. What we do is...unusual. I guess my dad made it a real vocation, a passion, and I like to believe, we get to make a difference. That we are a force for good."

"We are," he told her. "Your father would be so proud. I guess, in our lives, I can believe he is proud—somewhere in the great unknown, looking down."

"Thanks!" Danni said. "I like to think so," she whispered, and she curled back against him.

It was really late, and she was really exhausted. Despite that, she was afraid she wouldn't sleep with so many questions racing through her mind.

She barely laid her head on his chest before she was out, sound asleep.

***

Morning's light was just dimly breaking through the curtains when Quinn awoke with a start. He could feel Danni was no longer at his side. He bolted up, his heart racing.

But she was there.

He saw her at the desk, a pencil in her hand, a pad of the lodge's stationary before her. He knew she wasn't awake. It had happened before; Danni sleep walking—and sleep drawing.

She was really a wonderful artist; her scenes of New Orleans were becoming legendary. Colleen hadn't just wanted her work for the lodge because they were friends—Danni was good. Exceptionally good. She could somehow breathe life into a stationary scene.

This was something new, though. Ever since coming into her own as a collector of the bizarre and evil, she had taken to this sleep drawing upon occasion. He was careful, when they were home, to have a robe ready at all times, lest she wander downstairs at the house and shop on Royal Street in nothing but her birthday suit to sit down and sketch when they were in the midst of a case.

He walked over to her, looking over her shoulder to see what it was she was drawing.

A pendant.

He thought it was like the one he had seen on Daphne Alain. Maybe it was a little bit different; he wasn't sure. But it was detailed in every way, a drawing of an elegant pendant on a chain. The fleur-de-lis, a symbol for New Orleans and much of Louisiana.

Like the one on the woman in the picture from the book, she'd said.

She added a final touch and sat back in the chair at the desk, her eyes sightless. He knelt down before her, touching her knees, waking her gently.

"Danni, Danni!" he whispered softly.

She blinked; her eyes opened wide. She stared at the drawing on the desk and turned to him.

"Quinn! I...I was..."

"The pendant. I think we have found our talisman," he said. "But as Daphne told us, there could be hundreds of imitations around."

She shook her head. "Go to the house. Ask Billie to get to my dad's book. See what's in there. He may have had some experience with this...there are answers in the book."

She'd known nothing about her father's book until Angus had been dying.

He had to admit, he'd known nothing about it himself, but Angus—while trying to maintain a life of innocence for his daughter—had prepared for his death. He had catalogued many objects he'd come in contact with along with warnings about those he'd heard about—but never found.

He nodded.

"I'll take Billie the picture; he can get on it while I'm with Larue and driving back."

He drew her from the chair, holding her for a moment. But holding her wasn't a good idea—it could lead to other ideas.

"Go back to sleep," he told her.

"And you?"

"I'm going to get Larue and get going. I'll let you know as soon as we're on the way back. I'll come for you before meeting up with Trent Anderson."

She nodded solemnly.

"Danni, I—"

She set a finger to his lips. "Get going!" she told him, and she hurried back to the bed they'd shared, plunging beneath the covers.

He dressed quickly. When he had done so, he paused by the bed to say goodbye and smiled.

She was asleep.

He wasn't certain whether to be grateful—or slightly insulted and worried. He kissed her brow and headed out, her drawing of the fleur-de-lis medallion tucked into the files he carried beneath his arm.

He reminded himself cases were seldom solved in a day. Investigations could take weeks...months. Sometimes, they weren't solved. But this...

He wondered again if there had been someone who intended something evil against Daphne Alain the night before. If she might have been an intended victim. Maybe if they hadn't stayed to wait for her, they might have awakened to discover bodies had been set as scarecrows on the fairgrounds.

He didn't know. But he did believe this case didn't have months, weeks, or even days.

They had to solve it quickly.

If not...

Someone else was going to die.

No, two people would die. And once again, "scarecrows" would drip with blood.

Chapter 9

Danni was still half asleep when she heard her phone buzzing on the bedside table. She had set it on silent the night before, knowing the reverberation on the table would wake her anyway.

She quickly answered it, surprised to see by the caller I.D. that it was Billie McDougall—her father's assistant who had stayed on with her, and was an integral part of her shop on Royal Street, *The Cheshire Cat*—and of their lives. He really could star as Riff-Raff in a production of "The Rocky Horror Show." Perhaps as a crazed scientist in any version of "Frankenstein." But she loved him—he was like the great-uncle she never had.

"Billie! Hi!" She glanced at the time. Quinn couldn't possibly have gotten to New Orleans yet—he'd been gone less than an hour.

"Hey. Danni—"

"Quinn is bringing you a sketch. I need you to get into Dad's book in the basement. I'm trying to find out if a medallion—a stylized fleur-de-lis—might mean something. He'll—"

"Danni!" Bill interrupted, the soft burr of his voice strong. "Lass, he figured he wouldn't waste time. He took a picture of the drawing with his phone and texted it to me."

"Oh—of course. Why the hell didn't I just do it?"

"He said you were sleep-sketching. You were probably still half-asleep," Billie said.

"No excuse. But you're calling me. What did you discover?"

"I found Angus wrote a whole chapter on such objects and I read it," Billie said. "But even so, I recalled such a situation years ago. Years and years ago, when your father and I were in Ireland...he'd been called by a friend of your mom. People were dying horribly in County Cork. Seems they were plagued by a strange, antique brooch. But, lass, here's the thing—such an object only seems to be lethal in the wrong hands, which is why years and years had gone by before anything bad began to happen. Then this bloody bugger got ahold of it who had been thinking of doing-in his wife. She'd had the brooch, but he ripped it off her in a fight, and it seemed to do something to his mind. He killed her...and then set off on a murder spree when others questioned him, and well, suffice it to say, your dad figured it all out, we got hold of the brooch, and the killer still sits in prison. Ye'd feel sorry for the bugger, excepting that he'd been a wife-beater from the get-go and known to harass lasses and all. Anyway, Angus saw to it that the brooch was melted down, and the gold and the stones were buried about an old cemetery in so many places it could never be put back together again. You need to be getting hold of whatever that fleur-de-lis is, lass. Oh—and I looked into it, too. Naturally, lass, it will not be easy. The fleur-de-lis is so common a symbol here in New Orleans and all about the French areas of Louisiana. The one you drew has a special little curly-cue at the bottom petal—take a good look at it. That's what you're going to be looking for. Of course, like others, it's probably been copied, so be looking for the original, but I know you know that you must be looking for the right one."

"Thank you, Billie," Danni said. "Does that mean if a decent person—or a person just not capable of murder—gets their hands on it, then it's...nothing?"

"Exactly, lass, exactly," Billie told her.

"Thank you, Billie!"

"Take care, lass, take care."

"Always, Billie," Danni promised.

"Larue is taking Quinn by the murder site and the bed and breakfast where the poor murdered lass was staying, and then he'll be getting right back to you, you know!"

"Yes, thanks, Billie."

"No nothing crazy, eh, lass?"

"Nothing crazy," she promised, and bidding him goodbye, she ended the call, rolled over, and popped out of bed.

She had no intention of doing anything crazy. She just meant to be social.

Someone here had a cursed fleur-de-lis medallion. She thought it might have once been an innocent piece of jewelry, owned by Yvette—and turned at the time of her murder.

Copies were made to look like the real thing. But she hadn't been exposed to antiques all her life not to recognize the real from the fake.

As she finished dressing, the phone rang. It was Quinn. She grabbed it quickly.

"Where are you?" he demanded gruffly.

"In the room. I haven't headed out yet," she told him.

"Danni, Larue and I found an abandoned sedan—a car service sedan. We traced it back to a car service."

"What service?"

"A place called 'Fleur-de-lis Limo Corporation.' Danni—the company traces back to a major holding company. A company held by another company and that company owned by—"

"Trent Anderson," she said.

"Right. Larue has called Peter Ellsworth. Ellsworth is going to be picking Trent Anderson up now. We're starting to believe the man killed at the cemetery was the driver, but we don't know that for sure yet. None of the drivers have been reported missing—and the car wasn't scheduled out. Anyway, I'll let you know more as soon as I know anything."

"Is Trent Anderson being arrested?" Danni asked.

"Brought in for questioning. There's no direct evidence he had anything to do with it."

"But...he's local, he's...rich. He could pull it all off!"

"Yes, Danni, and there's no law that says you get to arrest a guy because he's local and rich. He's a person of interest, but nothing solid suggests his guilt."

"Okay, well, did you talk to Billie? See if he has a fleur-de-lis medallion, necklace, or not a necklace anymore just the medallion."

"Yes, I talked to Billie. Danni, there is no guarantee it is Trent Anderson, though I hope they're going to keep him for at least twenty-four hours. Stay careful, right?"

She sighed softly. "Of course. You, too."

"You got it."

The call ended. She stared at the phone and then headed out into the hallway.

To her great surprise, she almost ran right into Trent Anderson, who was just closing the door to a room down the hall as she was hurrying along.

***

They had barely left the area before Quinn saw the car.

It had been shoved into a canal of Bayou Teche—though the brush growing around it was high, the water hadn't been high enough to cover it completely.

Quinn was somewhat surprised he'd seen it at all, other than they'd expected the car had been abandoned somewhere, either that or—since no one had gotten a plate number off it—it had simply been driven back to where it had come from and gone back into service.

While Larue reported to Ellsworth, Quinn crawled through the swampy ground and into the water, determined to get a plate number and search for the ornament old John Appleby had described.

The plate number was easy enough.

The ornament was gone.

Larue reported the plate number; a tow truck was being sent out. CSI would go over the vehicle, though Quinn doubted they would get much from it.

They stood by Quinn's car, staring at the water and the car.

"Trent Anderson is a local—guess he'd be up on all the legends," Larue said. He looked at Quinn. "And—like anyone else—he could have gotten from NOLA and out here easily enough. Two murder scenes, two nights." He let out a sigh. "Guess we're lucky there weren't a few murders last night. What the hell is this, Quinn? If it's not Trent Anderson, do we have to worry about every cemetery in the country? A sick idiot killing people and disinterring them."

Quinn leaned on the car, looking over at Larue. "Here's what bothers me, which is why I wanted to get into New Orleans. Ally Caldwell was associated with Colleen's site and lodge. The young woman killed in New Orleans was also on that site. I want to see the room where she was staying—and talk to her landlady. Also, the woman who still lives at the mansion—all that was done in her cemetery and she didn't hear a thing? Why no security cameras?"

"There are cameras in the house—but not on the grounds. Sure, cemetery vandalism takes place, but most small museums or historic homes, the money spent on that kind of security isn't worth it. Most people don't wake up planning on killing people and hiking them up on poles in a cemetery."

Quinn nodded; he saw a car driving to their position, pulling off the road. It was Peter Ellsworth; a tow truck wasn't far behind him.

He strode toward them, eyeing the car in the marshy water.

"Trent Anderson isn't at his home," he said. "I have officers on the lookout for him; we'll bring him in for questioning. You know, though, unless I have some evidence that places him—not a company—at a murder site, I can't hold him more than twenty-four hours. Do you have anything more? Anybody get anything out of the car company in NOLA?"

"The car should have been in the lot. There were no drivers assigned to it on the night Ally disappeared," Larue told him.

"Well planned," Quinn murmured.

"And still making no sense to me," Larue said, staring at Quinn.

He really didn't want to know a fleur-de-lis medallion might have made a not-so-nice person into a lethal person. Quinn just shook his head, because it really wasn't making sense yet to him, either.

"What do we do from here?" Larue asked Quinn.

Peter Ellsworth nodded toward Quinn, indicating his sopping and muddied clothing.

"I'm thinking Quinn might want a shower and a change," Ellsworth said.

"In NOLA," Quinn said. "It's important that I talk to a few people there."

"You want to take a two-hour drive—" Larue began.

"Yes." Quinn turned to Ellsworth. "You can definitely hold on to him for twenty-four hours once you have him? His money and his clout won't get him out? We can do what we need to do and be back here in six hours."

"Go," Ellsworth said. "If I have to sit on him myself, he'll be at the station. Assuming, of course, that we find him."

"Let's move then," Quinn told Larue. He nodded to Ellsworth, "and thanks."

"Hey—I want this damned thing solved to. Preferably, before we have any more corpses!"

***

"Danni!"

Trent Anderson seemed sincerely glad to see her.

"Hey, Mr. Anderson, nice to see you," she managed.

Wasn't he supposed to be with the police by now?

"Mr. Anderson? Please, Danni, this is a place where we're all supposed to become friends," he said. "Trent. Just Trent. I'm glad to run into you."

They were alone in the hallway. She wasn't feeling particularly comfortable.

"Would you have some coffee with me?" he asked.

"Sure." *The coffee bar, yes, surrounded by people.* "I would love coffee right now!"

"I heard you and Mr. Quinn wanted to talk to me."

"You heard that already?"

"Of course. Police were out to take a report from Daphne Alain last night, and I'm the one who owns the fairgrounds; and my company hires the managers, makes the arrangements...all that. Anyway, I think you're right."

They were in the elevator then. Alone. He hit the button for the ground floor.

"We're right?" Danni asked.

He nodded somberly.

The elevator "pinged" and the doors opened. He held the door, letting her precede him. She stepped out, and he came to her side as they walked to the coffee bar together greeting others they passed on the way.

"Let me get the coffee. What would like?" he asked her.

She smiled. "Coffee. Just coffee."

She took a table. People were leaving the line with their cups of espresso, mochas, and lattes; many smiled nervously her way, some greeted her.

She heard bits of chatter, some talking about their arrangements for the ball, some talking about friends who had chosen to leave, and some talking about the murders—considering them devil worship or something of the like.

Trent Anderson came to the table bearing two cups of coffee. He set hers down and sipped his own while taking his chair. Then he told her bluntly, "You two are entirely right, and I should have thought of it myself already."

"Thought of—"

"The scarecrows," he said. "I'm having them taken down today. I mean, God knows, this horrible crazy person might have gone on to another city or town or even state by now, but...the scarecrows we have up might have looked like some kind of an invitation to him. If he's still around. They're being taken down—and being taken out of the horror house as we speak."

"That's great," Danni said. "Thank you."

"This is my home. The creepy scarecrows were always a part of the harvest—to ward off evil," he said. "Someone twisted the hell out of it."

"People will always twist things," she murmured. She noted his hands; they weren't soft as she might have expected. He did keep his nails clean and short, but his hands would never give away the fact he probably didn't have to do any kind of manual labor if he didn't want to.

He was charming—and good looking. Which made her curious—beyond the fact they had discovered that the car that had picked up Ally Caldwell had belonged to one his companies-within-a-company.

"You're smiling. Crookedly. Very attractive and slightly sexy, if I may say without sounding like some kind of a masher," he told her. He lifted his cup to her. "Trust me, I wouldn't ever want to tangle with your Mr. Quinn."

"I was just thinking that you, Trent, are a very attractive man. As such, it does seem a little strange you're on a dating site—any dating site."

He smiled at that. "*Let's Meet* is the only site I'm on. This is a small community," he told her. "I really like what Colleen Rankin is doing; you can chat online, but you can come to one of her get-togethers, too. None of that dating where you head to pick someone up and discover they're not a thing like their picture and not a word they wrote about themselves was true. Through Colleen's site, you can chat and then meet at a mixer and find out if what you thought while engaged with someone online was true. Plus you can also find out if there is any chemistry between you."

"I suppose that's what most people like about the site."

"Take Ally Caldwell—and not to speak ill of the dead. She was a beautiful woman, but man, she had one of the harshest personalities I've ever come across, and I work with a lot of high-powered business women in many different areas."

"You knew Ally?"

"Well, I met her."

"When?"

"Colleen was down in her New Orleans office with members of the staff before they came out here for the event. I saw her there. I can't say I knew her. But..."

He paused, looking downward sheepishly for a moment. "I did think she was a beautiful woman. I guess I was a little flirtatious when I talked to her. But...then she looked me up and down and looked me up and...she was hostile at first, and then strange, as if she'd checked out my financial status. I backed away and ran home as fast as I could."

"Did you meet Tracy Willard then, too?"

He smiled, sitting back. "Briefly, but we really started chatting at the mixer, and things moved on from there." He lowered his voice, moving closer. "I think she's afraid she wasn't supposed to be doing any mixing. I think she's wrong. Colleen is delightful, and she's one of the very few completely sincere people I think I've ever met."

"So that's still going well. You and Tracy? That's why you're here, at the lodge?" Danni asked.

He laughed softly. "I took a room here myself. Best to have one's own space. I like Tracy; she's lovely and a great deal of fun, but I'm not ready to commit to anyone. This is all very new." He was quiet another minute. "I don't think of myself as any kind of a mess, Danni, but I inherited money, and then I did well with it. While I don't think the world is out to get me, I've been around the block a bit. I wanted to be wanted for me, like anyone else, and not my money."

"Of course," Danni said. "We're all human."

He grinned, running his finger over the edge of his paper coffee cup. "I'd like to have what you and Mr. Quinn have one day."

"Oh?"

He gave her a crooked grin. "You communicate without words; you look across a room for one another and find one another. You didn't meet on a dating site, did you?"

She shook her head. "No, but...it wasn't an instant thing, trust me. We were ready to battle at the start."

"How did you get together?"

"Um, he had worked with my father. I met him when my father passed away."

"Oh, I'm sorry. I mean, I'm sorry about your father. I guess I'm glad for Quinn. Oh—and sorry for the rest of the lonely bachelors out here—not a pick-up line, I swear it!"

"Hey, you two, may I join you?"

They both looked up. Colleen had a cup of coffee and was standing by the table. She looked better than she had looked the day before; she was finding her strength.

"Of course!" Danni said. Trent leapt to his feet to pull out a chair for her.

"Are you ears ringing?" he asked Colleen.

"In a good way—or not so good?" Colleen asked. "I'm sorry; I'm trying, but..."

"In a wonderful way," Trent said. "I was telling Danni that yours is the only site I'm on. I think your way of thinking is brilliant!"

Colleen flushed. "Thank you. I just...I did think I was doing a good thing."

Trent Anderson took her hand. "Don't ever doubt that, Colleen. What happened here is not your fault; and you mustn't stop doing what you do because of an evil, sick person. They'll find whoever did this; I'm so sorry about Ally, but don't you stop."

She smiled sadly at him and then frowned, rising.

"Detective Ellsworth," she murmured. "He must know something; he's coming here."

Ellsworth was coming straight toward them.

Trent rose as Colleen did, and naturally Danni followed suit.

"Mr. Anderson," Detective Ellsworth said, "we need you."

"Me?" Trent asked. He seemed honestly surprised.

"We have some questions for you—if you wouldn't mind?"

The detective was unerringly polite; there was still something about his manner. There was no reason for him to have to tell Trent he would be coming—of his own volition or by force.

"I...sure. If I can help," Trent said.

"Wait! Detective Ellsworth, what is this?" Colleen protested.

Trent Anderson wasn't going to let it become a scene. He turned quickly to Colleen. "Please, Colleen, it's fine. I truly am happy to be of assistance in any way. I'll see you later. Danni, thanks for the chat. Mr. Quinn is truly a lucky fellow."

"Thanks!" Danni said. "And yes, of course, we'll see you later."

Her words were sincere, but she winced inwardly.

He was now connected to whatever had happened to Ally and the other murdered man. Something had to have been going on for a driver to have slipped into a limo service, taken a car, picked Ally up, and brought her to the cemetery to have her throat slit.

It was—through no matter how many channels—his limo company

He might well be a murderer.

"What's that all about?"

Danni and Colleen swung around. Tracy Willard had come upon them, her hands on her hips, and a serious frown on her face as she watched Detective Ellsworth and Trent Anderson leave.

"The police want to talk to Mr. Anderson," Colleen said.

"But why? He's the nicest guy in the world! He couldn't have anything to do with anything—and I...I know he couldn't have had anything to do with the murders!"

"I don't think he did either," Colleen said. "But, Tracy!" she added in a whisper. "How can you be so sure?"

"Because he was with me," Tracy admitted. "He couldn't have killed anyone. He was with me."

***

Quinn decided they'd stop at the MacDonald Mansion on the way into the city. Their drive was basically west to east, and it was easiest to stop at the border of the city first.

Problem was he wasn't dry. He was damp. Larue suggested they could get to the city and go to his home on Royal Street first, but Quinn didn't want to waste time.

His shoes squeaked when he walked, but he was mostly presentable.

The MacDonald Mansion was open for tours when they arrived; a pleasant girl at the ticket office started to tell them the times the next tours would start, but Larue quickly produced his I.D. and told her that he needed to see Fiona MacDonald.

She nodded gravely, picked up a phone, and made a call.

A moment later a woman of about thirty with her hair and dress in antebellum fashion appeared. She was grave as she hurried out to the porch to meet them, shaking hands with Larue whom she already knew and then Quinn.

"I would say we should go to the parlor, but the house is open and there are people visiting and guides giving tours. I could suggest a walk in the cemetery and garden, but you police still have it cordoned off. Which is fine, of course, just fine!"

"Well, we need to get out there anyway," Quinn said, "if you don't mind. And Detective Larue has the authority to lift the crime scene tape."

She winced. "I just hate going out there now," she murmured. "Once upon a time...I loved it. This may sound creepy, but I love my family history, and I love this house. I even loved they made a beautiful garden area out of family graveyard or cemetery. I guess it's more of a cemetery—we have some interments in the ground, but they started building vaults out here even before they had opened St. Louis #1. I know where I'll be one day, and honestly, it's comforting rather than creepy. Well, I did love it, but, now..."

They headed down the porch steps and around the house, through a trellis path and into what was a truly beautiful big of acreage—flowering trees had been planted and benches had been distributed throughout.

There were, however, three large pits in the midst of several above-ground single coffin tombs.

"CSI has everything," Larue murmured. "The morgue has the bodies; and our crime scene investigators have everything else."

Quinn headed straight for the three pits. "And the bodies were in the same order as in Perryville, right? Already deceased, the young woman, and then the man?"

"Right," Larue said.

Quinn turned to look back at the house. The attic rose above the neighboring trees.

"You saw nothing?" he asked Fiona MacDonald.

She shook her head, her expression distressed. "Mr. Quinn, that attic window there—it's not exactly where I sleep. That's a salon area and by bedroom is behind it. I sleep with the television on. I like the company of the voices. I live here alone. I've never been afraid before, and I don't really need to be afraid now. We have a great security system as far as the house goes. I'm truly horrified I didn't see what was happening. This is my business or my family's business, but it's also my home. And what was done here...like I said, it's my home." She offered them a dry expression, her lips curving downward. "It has been good for business. I had to call in guides who are usually off today."

"I guess 'haunted' history does do well," Larue murmured.

"Miss MacDonald, would you have heard anything going on before you went to bed?" Quinn asked her.

She nodded fervently. "Our last tour is later than most. Six o'clock. People don't leave until seven or eight, and they're welcome to walk around back here until they're ready to go. Milly Sturbridge, who manages the ticket counter, never leaves until about eight. She's an old family friend, and she's welcome to eat here, relax here, and leave when she's ready. That night, I had been out with friends. I came home about eleven. Nothing was amiss then. I was awake until midnight, and then I went to bed."

Quinn hesitated and then drew out his phone, thumbing to a picture of Allison Caldwell.

He moved quickly past the crime scene photo of her on the scarecrow and searched for one sent to him along with others from Peter Ellsworth's office. It took a minute; he knew Larue was looking at him curiously.

"Sorry," he said quickly. He found a picture of Allison Caldwell in life at last. "Miss MacDonald, by any chance, was this woman ever here?"

She stared at the picture a minute. "So many people come," she murmured, studying the picture and frowning. Then she nodded looking at him. "Maybe, I think so, yes. I think she was with a group of people, and...in fact, yes, I think it was her. I noticed her here because others were listening to the guide and enjoying the house and...she looked impatient. Anxious to be gone. She was an attractive woman with very dark hair. I was heading upstairs for something; she wasn't in my group. In fact—it was just a day or two before...before the murders here. Is she...a suspect."

He shook his head. "I'm sorry; she was a victim."

"Oh!" Fiona said, her face taking on a look of horror.

"You were shown a likeness of the woman, Belinda Cardigan, who was killed here, right?" he asked.

She nodded, swallowing hard, as if she was feeling ill.

"I'm truly sorry," he said.

"Yes, of course, Quinn, she saw pictures," Larue murmured.

"Had you seen her before?" he asked.

She shook her head and whispered, "No. But a lot of people come here. I have three full-time guides and a few college kids who cover when people are on vacation. I am here most of the time. When I'm not being a guide myself, I work on the books or sometimes have friends in. I mean, I live here, too. On certain days, we serve iced tea or lemonade and cookies, which I bake."

Quinn glanced at Larue. "We got pictures of our victim around," he said. "I'm afraid they weren't all certain if they had or hadn't seen Belinda."

Quinn nodded. "Thank you," he told her.

He walked over to the area where the earth had been dug out for the poles. He hunkered down picking up a piece of straw.

He'd seen the pictures of the crime scene here—and what had happened in Perryville had been just about a carbon copy.

He kept the piece of straw; he didn't honestly know if crime scene technicians could discover if it had been the same straw used at both places, but he wanted to find out.

Walking back to Larue and Fiona MacDonald who waited watching in silence, he nodded to Larue and told Fiona, "I'm truly sorry; we do intend to catch this killer."

"Of course. Really, I am happy to help. It's just so...so horrible."

"Yes," he said simply. "Well, we thank you very much."

"Ready?" Larue asked.

"Ready."

They headed back to the street where Quinn had parked.

"We do have a bunch of that at the lab," Larue told Quinn, noting the straw in his hand as they left.

"Yeah, but I thought we should take one back with us," Quinn said.

Larue shrugged. "Okay, their lab, our lab..."

"Comparison, up close and personal," Quinn said.

"And now, a shower for you and a change of clothing? Maybe something cold from the refrigerator at the house on Royal for me while I wait?"

"Almost," Quinn said.

Larue groaned. "You want to go to the bed and breakfast first?"

"I do."

"How can you stand yourself? You're wearing mostly-dried swamp water? Better still, how the hell does Danni stand you."

"Well, I don't usually wear nearly-dried swamp water, and if you were Danni, I just might shower first. But," he shrugged, grinning, "you're not Danni. What's the name of this place by the way?"

"*The Saint on St. Peter's,*" Larue said. "Hey—I didn't name the place. But let's go. I guess we're not far now, and we'll be in the French Quarter and can head to Royal Street then—if you do want to shower and stop by the place before returning."

Quinn nodded. "Yes, I do want to shower before another two-hour drive. For now."

"Onward," Larue said. He was quiet a minute. "What do you think it might mean—that Allison Caldwell was at that place, too?"

"It means she was there. 'With a group.'" Quinn said. "That, in itself, is not a surprise, because Colleen's people were in New Orleans for several days before heading out to the lodge. And I'm assuming, some guests or clients checked in at the office in the CBD here. What I find curious is this has been all over the news, and no one from Colleen's group mentioned having been here. Doesn't that strike *you* as odd?"

"Yes, now you've pointed it out. I never directly asked anyone that question. Oh, wait, I didn't really do any of the questioning out in Perryville; I had to leave that to the appropriate authorities—oh, and you," he added dryly. "To be honest, I wouldn't have thought to ask Fiona MacDonald if she'd ever seen Ally Caldwell. First, we know eye-witness reports can be skewed and sketchy at best. Downright wrong sometimes, too."

"And sometimes, right on," Quinn said. "Come on. Let's get to the bed and breakfast."

\

Chapter 10

If Colleen was upset because one of her employees had been acting like a client—with one of her most important clients—she didn't say so.

She simply frowned.

"If that's the case, and the police are suspecting Trent Anderson had anything at all to do with these horrendous murders, you must head to the station straight-way and tell them you know he's innocent, you're a witness, and Mr. Trent couldn't possibly have committed the killings!"

Danni remained silent. She and Quinn had seen Tracy and Trent together that morning, and it certainly seemed as if they'd spent the night together. At least, they were together then.

Still, the car having come from his company was still something that needed to be explained. Perhaps the police having Trent at the station would, at the least, allow them to talk to him, and perhaps, if he sincerely wanted to help, Trent Anderson might be able to give them some answers.

She decided not to insist Tracy get right in and tell the police what she knew.

"Colleen, I'm sure Trent will tell them he was with someone, that he has a witness, and they'll believe in his innocence. But Detective Ellsworth did just say they had some questions; we should probably let them talk. If Mr. Anderson begins to feel he's being pressured, I'm sure he has a half dozen lawyers who can get in there for him. Right now, I'm sure he just wants to help."

Both women looked at her. Even Colleen, who had appeared so indignant and sure, had begun to look thoughtful and concerned.

"Okay, then, if they arrest him, we'll all go in," Colleen said. "I mean, he is such a nice guy; he might allow himself to be arrested rather than tell the truth."

Danni didn't think even a nice guy was going to cop to a murder rap rather than admit he'd been sleeping with a woman, but for the moment she smiled.

Then she frowned feeling every muscle in her body tighten. Colleen was wearing a necklace. The medallion on it was a fleur-de-lis. Just about a perfect copy of the one she had sketched that morning.

"What?" Colleen asked, looking at her worriedly.

"Nothing. Just out of context here when we're worrying about someone. I just noticed your necklace. That's so pretty. Did you get it out here—I mean in Perryville rather than New Orleans?"

Colleen self-consciously fingered the necklace. "Yes, I bought it at the fair. That harvest fair they have going on. It's...it's just pretty. It's a good fake, but they aren't real stones and it's just gold-plated. Would you like it? You're welcome to it, Danni. Giving you the necklace would be the least that I could do for you, with all the help you and Quinn have given me."

"No, no, I don't want to take your necklace, but I'd love to borrow it," Danni said.

"Sure!" Colleen took the necklace off and handed it to Danni.

Danni smiled. "Thanks," she said.

"People were killed; they've taken Trent, and you two are talking about a necklace," Tracy murmured.

"No more," Colleen said. "Excuse me. Albert Bennett is over at the counter. I need to speak with him. Tracy, we're going to have to work on some numbers, see how the ball is shaping up, how many people stayed, how many have left, if the band is still coming, and we need to bring those numbers to the kitchen."

"You want me to meet now, with you and Albert Bennett?" Tracy asked.

"Yes," Colleen said firmly.

"Larry Blythe really does the computers and the numbers," Tracy reminded her.

"Yes, and he'll be down soon. You need to meet with us," Colleen said. Then she smiled gently. "Tracy, it will help me and help you. Let's keep our minds occupied, okay?"

Tracy smiled. "But if they arrest Trent—"

"You, Danni, and I will head right to the station."

"How will we know what they're doing?" Tracy asked anxiously.

Colleen looked at Danni. "You can call Quinn, right? He'll know what's going on."

Danni nodded. "He's in New Orleans right now, but he's in touch with Peter Ellsworth."

Tracy was staring at her. "You knew! You knew they were coming for him."

"I wasn't surprised," Danni said. "They need to talk to him; he really might be able to help. His property is next to the cemetery. He may know things that can help he just might not think about unless he's speaking with people who know the right questions."

"See?" Colleen asked. "Oh, there's Larry now. He's smiling and coming our way."

"He looks like he finally got himself a girl—horrors! Maybe he even got to have sex!" Tracy said.

"Hey!" Colleen protested. "Larry is a hard-working and very nice man," she said.

"Sorry. He is a great co-worker," Tracy said. "I'm just...I'm just nervous and being tacky, I guess. I like Larry, but let's face it, he's not exactly a hunk. Oh, sorry again. I'm beginning to sound like Ally—oh!" She realized what she had said and clamped her hand over her mouth, looking at Colleen wide-eyed. "Oh, how terrible! I'm so sorry. I almost forgot—"

"It's hard to believe she's gone," Colleen said.

Larry had reached them. Danni thought he purposely forced his smile to fade as he met his employer, remembering they had just lost a colleague.

And a friend. At least to Colleen.

"Good morning," he said, joining them. "Are we meeting here, Colleen? I thought it was going to be up in your suite? I was just going to grab some coffee. We did hire great people for this coffee bar, didn't we? And such good coffee!"

"So, who were you with last night?" Tracy asked him, smiling.

Larry turned red. "I—I—"

"It's all right," Colleen said. She let out a sigh. "I'm all for love! If you found someone, I'm very happy for you."

"I think she likes me," Larry said.

Albert Bennett came striding over from the coffee bar just catching the last. "Larry! The pretty brunette you were with last night? I saw her talking to you, and yes, I'd say she likes you. I looked on her page—she loves computers and gadgets—she's perfect."

"Well, we talked. I mean, I can't say it's a perfect relationship, but...there might be something there. And I'll be able to see her! When we head back to base. She's—"

"A New Yorker," Albert said.

Larry nodded, studying his co-worker and smiling slowly. "She is pretty...more like your kind of girl."

"She was all over you, buddy," Albert said. "All over you—give yourself some credit, my friend, you're educated, slim and fit—a catch."

"We're meeting in the suite, guys, now," Colleen said. She smiled, taking any sting out of her words. Then she looked at Danni. "My friend, you're welcome to join us—"

"Thank you, thank you. I need to run back up to my room. I'll leave you all be, and see you later!"

She smiled, gave them all a small wave, and headed for the elevator. In her room, she checked to see the balcony doors were securely locked and then double checked the door to the hallway. She checked her phone to make sure she hadn't missed a call from Quinn.

She sat at the desk then and pulled out the necklace that Colleen had given her.

A copy, just as Colleen had said.

She set the necklace down and picked up one of the books on the area and the legends and scanned the information quickly. She found herself turning back to the book that had been written in the early twentieth-century. It seemed to engross her the most. The author, having read through letters of the time—like checking someone's texts these days Danni thought—had another theory on the murder.

Yvette had not been killed by her lover's mother. Rather, Yvette had been killed by a rival for Percival's attentions. It was an interesting theory. But if that were the case, who had murdered his mother at a later date, starting the legend that her spirit awoke now and then to destroy such women? And how did any of this relate to the number three?

There was an answer. Percival's mother had tried to prove her own innocence.

Perhaps the real killer had been getting too close.

Danni was so engrossed in her reading the knock on her door caused her to jump.

She rose, shaking her head at the unease that filled her. All she had to do was go to the door—and check out the peephole.

She was safe. Locked in her room.

She rose and headed silently to the door.

***

The French Quarter in New Orleans was bordered by Canal Street, Rampart Street, Esplanade, and the Mississippi River—it took Quinn and Larue a few minutes to reach their destination from the MacDonald Mansion right on the edge of the city where New Orleans meet up with Metairie.

The French Quarter was home, but they weren't heading for Royal Street yet. They were heading to a destination right off Rampart—across from the Treme area, and just blocks from St. Louis #1, and for that matter, St. Louis #2. They passed by the beautiful and historic church Our Lady of Guadalupe, built in 1826 and serving as a mortuary chapel during the yellow fever that ravaged the city at the time—a place from which mourners bringing a corpse could easily reach St. Louis #1.

"Jazz mass," Quinn murmured.

"Amazing and, yes, I've been!" Larue assured him. "St. Peter Street just ahead!"

"What, you don't think I know where I'm going?" Quinn asked.

The bed and breakfast Belinda Cardigan had chosen for her stay was a charming old house built soon after the fires that ravaged New Orleans in 1788 and 1794—when the French Quarter had been largely rebuilt with the Spanish having dominion over the area at the time.

It was a typical and inviting place, much like the house on Royal Street where Angus Cafferty had opened his "Cheshire Cat," and where Danni and their crew continued to run it.

There was a handsome courtyard surrounded by a stone fence. The entry to the bed and breakfast was through the iron gates that led into the courtyard, and then onto the patio where double-French door opened into the first room.

The manager of the "Saint on St. Peter's" was an older woman with soft, silver-white hair, dark brown eyes and a quick smile.

Her smile faded when she saw it was Jake Larue coming into her patio heading to meet her where she sat behind a desk watching her computer.

"Mrs. Robertson," Larue said, "I'd like you to meet Mr. Quinn. He's—"

"Mr. Quinn!" Mrs. Robertson said, rising to shake his hand. "I know of you," she said softly, and then shrugged. "I'm friends with Billie McDougal. I've known him forever."

"Oh," Quinn said, wondering just what it meant that she might know about him. "It's a pleasure to meet you, and I'm surprised, really, that we haven't met yet."

"Ah, well, when you reach the great ages as Billie and I have discovered, a wild night on the town means bedtime is nine instead of eight. I'm not getting out much these days, but Billie and I, we keep up. And Detective Larue, I'm happy to speak with you both. I have, however, spoken with the police. I wish I had something for you. Miss Cardigan was such a lovely girl. So friendly and absolutely sweet! Anyone staying here when she was a guest was bowled over by her. We serve breakfast in the courtyard you just came through. Unless it's raining, of course, then we're in here. Of course, that doesn't matter to you two men right now at all, does it? What can I do to help you?"

"You knew nothing about where she was going?" Quinn asked.

Mrs. Robertson shook her head. "She didn't say, but she had rented a car. She was in love with the city and anxious to go beyond. She did say she was heading west. I took that to mean she was maybe going to drive out to Texas. She did mention she loved Austin and went whenever she could. She...she talked to other guests. I had two couples with children staying here, and she was wonderful with them. Truth was, she had checked out...before she was found. She was here just a couple of days seeing the historic sites in a swift hurry, loving everything she saw. I tell you, such a heinous crime is always tragic, but that such a beautiful young woman was taken...so sad."

"Mrs. Robertson, did she say anything about a dating site to you?" Larue asked her.

Mrs. Robertson shook her head. "No...she was lovely. I doubt she needed to be on a dating site."

"Did she mention a harvest ball or anything like that?" Quinn asked.

Again, Mrs. Robertson shook her head. "No...seemed to be on her own. Except that one night when she was here..."

She paused, thoughtful. "Well, one night when she was here, I believe she...well, met someone, a man. I happened to wake up, and my window is right up there..." She pointed above herself at the ceiling. "There's a balcony, and I know I shouldn't, but I often leave my windows open once the temperature cools down a bit. I know I heard her voice, and I think...I think she might have been talking to a man. Laughing. She sounded happy." She paused again, wincing. "I don't like to say because I'm not sure. I mean, voices were just drifting up to me, you know?"

"Please, we'll remember you weren't certain about what you heard," Quinn said.

"They might have been making arrangements to see each other at another time—at another place. It sounded as if they hadn't known each other long, but they liked one another. The next morning, she didn't say anything about meeting a new friend or heading out to meet anyone. She left the morning after that."

"What about your other guests?" Quinn asked.

"Well, of course, the police asked about that, too. They spoke with a few people, but while she was charming and played with the children here, she didn't say anything about where she had come from or where she was going. When she talked to them, it was always about things they should see and do in New Orleans. They must take a carriage ghost tour, do the museums on Jackson Square—oh, and have beignets and café au lait at Café du Monde! How they need to take their kids to the aquarium and the zoo. She wasn't a gambler, but she had walked through Harrah's and had a great steak dinner there."

They stayed a few minutes longer; Quinn complimented her on the bed and breakfast, and gave her his card, asking she get a hold of him should she think of anything—anything else at all.

"I wish I could help!" she said.

"You did help," Quinn assured her.

As they headed back to the car, Larue asked, "I like to believe every step brings us closer to a solution, but...what do you think we gained here?" he asked.

"We know she was a member of Colleen's dating site. I believe she did go into the office here in the Central Business District, if only for a minute. She met someone who had to do with the dating site, and I believe she was heading out to Honeywell Lodge for the event there. She was heading west. If she was with a man...he might well have been her killer."

"Right," Larue said, "but which one? You think it was Trent Anderson, that he came into the city and killed Belinda, dug up a corpse, and killed another man—here. Then did the same back in Perryville? I can see Perryville, but...how and when did he dig up or disinter a corpse here? Did he pack the straw in his vehicle? It's just crazy."

"It's crazy complicated whoever did it," Quinn said. "Come on, you can get your cold drink at the house on Royal while I take a shower before you are forced to take the long drive back with me at your side."

Larue looked upward. "Thank the Lord!" he said fervently.

***

Danni opened her door. It was Colleen who stood on the other side.

"Hey," she said. "How did your meeting go?" she asked.

Colleen walked into the room, dropping her shoulder bag on a chair and flopping down on the bed. "Fine. We're going to go on. Apparently, we're more popular than ever." Her voice had a bitter note to it. "If only I'd known the horrible murder of a friend would have made me more popular than shrimp and grits, I might have thought of it earlier."

"Colleen," Danni said gently. "It just means people have heard about the site now and—"

"And they're ghoulish. I feel like shutting down, except I just opened this, and I was with Albert and Tracy and Larry, and if I let things fall apart now...there is so much invested! I'll go down like a ton of bricks."

"You're not going to go down. Colleen, terrible things happen. People have been killed in hotel rooms, restaurants, and malls—but the businesses can't close down. You're...you're going to pick up and go on. I know you're seriously mourning Ally, and you should get to mourn her. You have a right to cry and be furious. But, at this time, really, trust me...the responsibility of going on will be something important to you and something that will really help you."

Colleen nodded then shook her head. "I'm so naïve. I set up a dating site plus a meeting and event venue for clients...and all my employees are fooling around all over the place. I blithely had no idea! My plan here is for people to really find romance!"

"Well, I think Tracy is crazy about Trent Anderson, and apparently, he enjoys her company."

"Ally slept with anyone she found to be exceptionally attractive—if and only if she felt the urge. I never knew Tracy...well, you know what? Maybe I thought they were both a little too frisky with Albert Bennett, but...oh, I don't know! What difference does it make? I wanted this to be a site where people really found romance and relationships—not a shack-up site!"

Danni was silent.

Colleen sighed. "If only—" she said and broke off. Her phone was ringing, and she angled around on the bed to get into her pocket to find it and answer it.

"Yes, yes, yes, of course!"

She ended the call and leapt off the bed. "I've got to go," she said.

"Where?"

"John Appleby—he wants to speak to me. He doesn't want to come here."

"So, where do you think you're going?"

"He—he—said he was afraid to be here. Walls have ears, he said. I'll be back—way before our social mixer this evening. I promise."

She headed for the door; Danni blocked her way.

"Where?" she demanded.

"Oh, at the cemetery gates."

"You shouldn't be in that cemetery, Colleen."

"I'm not going in the cemetery; I'm meeting him at the gates. Let me go, Danni! Do I need to call security on you, my friend? Please—I have to know what happened here! I can't go on if we don't find out what happened. Maybe Appleby will talk to me when he couldn't talk to others!"

"Colleen, they're questioning Trent Anderson right now."

"And he didn't do it! He was sleeping with Tracy."

"We'll get cops to go with us—"

"No! If he were going to talk to the cops, John Appleby would have done so by now. I know him, Danni. He did some odd jobs for me when I was out here on inspections while we were working on the final set-ups for the event!"

"Colleen, listen—"

"Damn it, I'm going!"

"You're not going alone."

"I'm going!"

"Then, I'm going with you."

She wasn't letting Colleen go alone.

She would go with Colleen and call Quinn on the way. If he was still an hour down the road, at least, he'd make sure Ellsworth saw to their safety.

Colleen was on a mission. She all but ran down the hall, ignoring the elevator, taking the stairs. Danni hurried after her, having to run to catch up with her as she made her way around the curve of the driveway to the parking area and her car.

For a minute, she was afraid Colleen wasn't going to let her into the car.

Then Colleen sighed. "You always could run pretty fast."

She opened the passenger door and Danni slid into the car.

She wasn't happy; this was foolish. She couldn't let her friend go alone.

Three...

Three corpses on three scarecrows.

One time, two times...

And she was certain, the killer was definitely intending there should be three.

Chapter 11

Admittedly, it was good to shower.

The slimy water had dried on him had made everything he had been wearing into a slimy mess that had dried on him weirdly—very uncomfortable. So, he showered quickly—with the speed of light, he had promised Larue—stepped out, and dressed quickly again. When he was clad, he hesitated. He hadn't been wearing his ankle holster or the small Smith and Wesson it carried. He had only been carrying his Glock, which fit nicely in a small holster he had between his waistband and the small of his back.

He decided to strap on the smaller weapon as well, and then hurried out.

Wolf—their aptly named hybrid dog, a beloved pet and guard dog he had acquired form a case several years ago—was waiting for him the hall. The great animal whined pathetically and thumped his tail on the floor.

"Hey, it was supposed to be a romantic event—and dogs weren't invited. Not my fault, I swear," he told the dog.

Wolf stood on his hind legs, balancing backwards as if he was a small terrier, seeking attention. In that position, the dog rose to about Quinn's height of six-foot-four.

"Get down and come here, you lug!" Quinn said, and the dog obediently did so, coming forward for some attention.

"We need to get downstairs, boy," Quinn told the dog and hurried past him, taking the stairs to the ground floor two at a time.

At the landing, a hallway led to the kitchen and from there out to the courtyard. If he took the hallway in the other direction, he'd pass Danni's artist's studio and then enter the shop.

He didn't enter the shop; he'd briefly greeted Bo Ray Jenkins, a young man now in recovery, whom they'd also met on a case. Father Ryan had helped Bo Ray, and he was now invaluable to them.

Exceptionally valuable today, because Quinn had Larue waiting in the kitchen with Billie McDougall, listening to anything Angus's old and experienced assistant might have to say.

He strode into the kitchen, Wolf at his heels. Larue and Billie were at the table. Billie had made sandwiches and Larue had already eaten a few evidenced by the crumbs on his plate.

"Sit down and eat, Quinn?" Billie said.

Quinn shook his head. "Can't take the time, Billie. I don't like being here when Danni is there; even if Ellsworth did find Trent Anderson and bring him in."

"He had the means, so it seems. Someone had to know him in New Orleans and Perryville—and the cemeteries and the legends," Billie said. "Except," he added, nodding toward Larue, "I think your suspect has an alibi for the time of the murder."

He glanced at Larue. "I got a call from the duty officer— apparently Tracy Willard came into the office, swearing Trent

Anderson had to be innocent. He'd been with her. She was ready to swear up and down he'd been with her all night."

Quinn, reaching into the refrigerator for a bottle of water, paused.

"She was with him in the morning," he said.

"Well, I've looked into your people," Billie said. "I've been searching the site and with a little help from some friends who wouldn't want to be caught hacking, I've been able to do some research. Now, every one of Colleen's top employees has been in and out of New Orleans—and out to Perryville—while setting up for this. So, you could be looking at one of them. But whatever this young woman says...I also looked into straw deliveries and the only one out there in that area, my good lads, who received a major shipment of straw is...you guessed it. None other than our good friend, Mr. Trent Anderson."

"Straw for—what?" Quinn asked.

"Besides scarecrows—and turning the dead into scarecrows?" Billie asked. "Horses. And no, he doesn't feed his animals straw—causes colic. He buys lots of grain and hay, too. Straw is used for bedding for his horses, in the stables he has at his place out there. Yeah, that lodge of his that's right by the cemetery."

"He invited Danni and me to see the place. Some time," Quinn said. "Should have rushed over right then. Still, it makes no damned sense."

"It may. There's more to the legend about that fleur-de-lis medallion or necklace or whatever," Billie said. "The one Danni sleep-drew." He frowned suddenly, glancing at Larue.

Larue just shook his head. "I don't believe any of this. But it seems to work for you all often enough, so...pretend I'm not here."

"Here's what I think," Billie said. "Danni saw that necklace on an historic drawing or an image of a painting. It had been worn by Yvette—Yvette of the legend we believe. Murdered Yvette. I think whoever killed her ripped the necklace from her."

"And she cursed the necklace, or the murderer, and the curse went on to the necklace?" Quinn asked.

Billie shrugged. "I don't see a spirit of a nice kid like Yvette supposedly was trying to cause all kinds of mayhem or murder. Now, after the woman who killed her was killed. I had a brief conversation with Danni earlier. I don't think the lover's mum was the one who murdered her—apparently, young Percival was a fine catch. He wound up marrying a 'right' girl, and she survived the marriage long enough to produce an heir, but she died a gruesome death herself. Harvest time, again. They'd been out celebrating. Her husband was distracted, everyone started to leave. Oh, go figure on this. I found a source—one that admits it's based on legend and not history—but supposedly, they were celebrating in the cemetery. Anyway, everyone leaves, and the wife winds up falling into a hole somewhere in the cemetery. When they finally found her, she'd been pretty well chewed by a lot of local wildlife. I'm guessing that means a lot of rats and bugs and birds were at her. I've yet to hear of a gator who could crawl straight up a grave prep site that was over six feet deep. Whatever, and I don't know if any of it is true. But she would have had the locket by then—wrenched off Yvette. Maybe Percival's mother was determined to prove her own innocence and wound up being attacked by the woman who became his wife. Maybe she cursed the necklace. Who knows? But apparently, it can only enhance a person's...capabilities."

"As in encourage murder?" Quinn asked. "Still...why?"

Larue spoke up. "Revenge, greed, power, money." He paused and looked at Quinn. "Insanity?" he suggested.

"We've got to get back," Quinn said. "Thanks, Billie. I swear, we'll keep in touch."

"And I'll keep at it," Billie promised.

Quinn and Larue headed out. In the courtyard, parking area, Quinn started to slip into the driver's side of the car. Before he could enter, Wolf came tearing out after him, barking insanely.

"Wolf!"

"He wants to go with you!" Billie called from the doorway.

"Wolf!" Craig said. But the dog wouldn't back down.

"Wolf, dogs just aren't invited."

Then again, did it matter if they were?

He looked at Larue.

"Hey," Larue said, "the dog smells better than you did when we were coming out here!"

Quinn cast his friend a stern glower, got out, and opened the back door for the dog. Wolf happily jumped in, and they were on their way.

***

"Colleen, you know this is crazy, don't you?" Danni asked. "We should turn around and head back. There has to be a coffee shop besides the one at the lodge somewhere in Perryville; we can meet John Appleby there. I can't believe he suggested to you that we meet at the cemetery."

Colleen glanced her way as she drove. "I think he just thought it up quickly. Maybe he was around other people or something. It was as if he just wanted to get off the phone."

"But you agreed. You said we should meet at the cemetery?"

"Okay, well, I started out thinking the fairgrounds, but there would be too many people there, and I knew he didn't want to come to the lodge because he didn't want to see people there, either, or be heard by people, or whatever. I was afraid he was going to hang up on me. I know Larue was going to meet with him here—and Quinn, I guess—but, even then, he didn't want to come in."

"It's crazy," Danni warned.

"Well, you shouldn't be in the car!"

Danni sighed. "How well do you know him?"

"You can't believe John Appleby is responsible for any of this, can you? I know I called on him before we were opening for all kinds of help. Things the major contractors left undone, a problem with the pool. When the company that installed the indoor pool said they couldn't make adjustments for a week, John helped. I believe he's a good man. Besides, we don't have to go crawling among the graves or anything—we'll meet at the archway."

Danni pulled out her phone.

"What are you doing?" Colleen demanded.

"Letting Quinn know what we're doing."

"Oh, Danni, please—I think he saw something, or knows something...we need to speak with him!"

"Don't worry; Quinn won't show up and ruin it all. He's far away at the moment; he headed out to New Orleans with Larue."

Quinn answered and warned right away, "I'm on speaker phone. Larue is with me."

"Great—that means you're driving; you're on your way back?"

"We are. Where are you?" he asked.

Danni glanced over at Colleen. "I'm with Colleen; we're going to have a chat with John Appleby."

"He knows something more—something he didn't tell me or the cops?"

"Colleen believes he does. Anyway, we'll talk to him. How was the house, or I should say, everyone at the house? And the trip—anything?" she asked hopefully.

"Billie thinks an historical killer got hold of the locket. He believes the killer murdered Yvette and stole her locket, and that killing Yvette and then the lover's mother—who was supposed to be blamed and is, by legend, blamed—is what cursed the locket. Yvette was good, I believe."

"Oh, yes, poor Yvette—she was sadly victimized. I read her diary. I would have liked her," Danni said.

"I don't get any of this, but watch out for lockets!" Larue said.

Danni smiled.

"What's going on?" Colleen asked.

Quinn was on speakerphone. Danni was not.

She shook her head for Colleen and covered her phone with her hand. "Nothing," she told Colleen. "Larue is...wishing he could hide his head in the sand."

"Oh," Colleen murmured.

"So, Appleby is coming to the lodge?" Quinn asked. "He wouldn't come in the other night."

"No, he's not coming to the lodge. We're going to meet him."

She didn't say where; she knew by the beat of silence that Quinn had guessed.

"At the cemetery? Danni, you're not going to the cemetery, are you?"

She didn't answer. She could see they had reached the cemetery; the arched gates to the place were rising just before them.

Crime scene tape still covered the gates and the gates were locked.

Which didn't mean a damned thing. The wall was so long and broken, the gates were seriously nothing more than a suggestion.

"Danni, where are you?" Quinn demanded.

"At the cemetery, but really, I don't think you need to worry. We're not going in. We'll talk out here on the road by the cars. Colleen is very afraid Appleby won't talk if he sees cops, that he's afraid he'll be misunderstood or mocked in any way...well, if he even has an idea of something, he'll only tell her because they're friends."

Colleen was starting to slow the car directly in front of the gates.

Danni could see John Appleby was there already; his truck was off the road and he was standing right at the archway waving to them.

She started to wave back and heard Quinn say softly, "Danni, did it ever occur to you Colleen might be involved in this?"

"No!" she told him, but she knew Quinn. If he wasn't almost here himself, he would understand what she was saying.

Have Peter Ellsworth send someone until you can get here—just in case.

And, no! She didn't believe Colleen might be involved. Someone near her, yes—but not Colleen!

"We're here; I can see John Appleby. I'm sure we're safe," she emphasized, knowing he knew her words signified what she wanted was to be safe. "I've got to go," she told Quinn, not waiting for a reply but ending the call.

Colleen braked the car. She took off her seatbelt and Danni did the same.

Colleen then turned and looked at Danni.

"See, I told you—it's all okay. John Appleby is right where he said he'd be."

Looking at her, Danni suddenly frowned. Her friend was wearing a chain again. Danni reached out to lift the chain— drawing out the medallion that had lain beneath her blouse.

It was another fleur-de-lis.

Something inside Danni quickened. "I thought you gave me yours last night."

Colleen laughed. "I told you these pieces were just costume. I bought a few of them; I was going to use them for little gifts for some of the staff. Hey, what the heck is going on with John—look at him, he's waving at us madly?"

Danni had time to turn and look and see John Appleby waving wildly, as Colleen had said, and looking as if he were seeing a giant tidal wave.

"He's warning us," she managed to say...and then, no more. Something slammed into Colleen's little rental car with a vengeance, like a bulldozer slamming against the wind. Danni had no time to brace herself. She went flying against the front windshield hard.

A twinkling of neon seemed to dance before her.

Then nothing, nothing at all.

***

"Get hold of Peter Ellsworth, please—fast!" Quinn said to Larue.

"Already dialing," Larue said, glancing Quinn's way. "You know, everything could be fine. The way we've figured it, Trent Anderson had the means and the ability. Hell, he even had straw delivered. He may live two hours out of New Orleans, but as we both know, that's nothing. Of course, there is the alibi—"

"He was with Tracy when we found the corpses. I assumed they'd been sleeping together somewhere. But she could have been lying. She could either be so enamored of his money she lied to protect him, or she really believes in his innocence. I wish I knew her better," Quinn said. "But it doesn't matter—"

Larue held up his hand; he had Peter Ellsworth on the phone. He briefly informed the man of what was going on, listened to the reply, and then said to Quinn, "How far do you think we are out from the area of the cemetery? I told him I thought we were about half an hour or so.

"That would be right," Quinn said, "But I can—and will—make it about twenty minutes."

***

Danni woke smelling something deep and disturbing. Like decaying foliage, raw earth, dank and wet.

She opened her eyes slowly and still, for a minute, the world spun. She closed her eyes again, but the smell was strong. She touched her forehead and felt something sticky.

Blood.

Then she remembered the crash. Well, it hadn't been a crash, per se. They had been run down by something hard and heavy, like a massive truck or even a car going at a speed meant to kill and if not kill...

Render one unconscious.

She became aware of the smell again and opened her eyes carefully, afraid to move. She stared straight at a broken-jawed skull. Some type of a crawling insect made its way out of one of the eye sockets. The smell came from the fact she was lying flat on the ground inside one of the hill vaults or tombs, one of the three. She was lying on earth and decay and straw.

She didn't move; she listened. She'd been in the car—suspecting Colleen. But Colleen had been in the car with her.

She had been hit just as hard, surely rendered unconscious, and perhaps dragged or carried into the cemetery somewhere as well.

Danni listened and listened.

Nothing.

She carefully moved checking her limbs. She was sore, but sore all over. She hadn't broken any bones. The way she had struck the dash and the windshield, she was damned lucky she had not crushed her nose right into her head. Luckily, she had not.

She managed to sit up as silently as possible and look around. She was alone in the tomb. But she had been with Colleen, and she had seen John Appleby waving at them, desperately trying to warn them of what was to come.

This was insane. She'd called Quinn. There would be a cop—or cops—out there somewhere!

The killer was growing bold. Night would come soon enough, but remnants of light must still be flooding the cemetery. She could see streaks of it just coming through the opening.

That meant she was in the first tomb, where the almost hidden crevice connected to the nature-claimed vaults of the cemetery.

Her mind raced, again focusing on Colleen. No. She couldn't believe in friend's guilt, but she knew, she had to consider any possible suspect. Collen had been out in the area often, she had been in New Orleans. She had gotten to know

Trent Anderson. She had access to everything about her own dating site.

No...

There would be no way she would have had the strength to ram the scarecrow poles into the ground; she could not have managed this on her own.

Maybe no one had managed this on their own; it was, at the least, a two-person effort.

She closed her eyes briefly, wincing. No.

Colleen was wearing another fleur-de-lis. A copy. There were dozens of them, so she said. What if Colleen had really befriended Trent Anderson herself, or...

Someone else.

But...

Trent. Trent Anderson. He had property right next to the graveyard.

But even assuming Colleen had an accomplice, would it have to be Trent?

She had to get out carefully. Find John Appleby—and Colleen. Easy enough; she knew to crawl out slowly and silently and use the tangle of foliage just outside to hide.

She got to her feet and swayed for a moment. She blinked hard and concentrated.

She had to move—had to!—if she wanted to survive and find Colleen and John Appleby.

Determined, she made her way past bones, coffins, tombs, and the dust and ash of the ages to the narrow, shrouded entrance to the tomb.

Carefully, she climbed out, staying low, keeping her body almost completely flat and one with the ground.

She immediately ducked behind the weeds and brush that all but covered the opening.

She almost gasped out loud but stopped herself by clamping a hand over her mouth.

There were three poles set up, one in front of each of the grass-covered vaults.

Piles of straw were set up by them, along with lengths of rope.

Three...

Ready for three flesh and blood bodies.

And she'd found John Appleby. He was lain right before the first of pole. She didn't know if he was dead or alive; she had to reach him and get help.

But before she could move, she heard it.

An eerie laughter, echoing through the graveyard, as if an evil witch from an old fairy tale had made an appearance.

It was no evil witch who had arrived, Danni knew.

It was the killer.

Chapter 12

"We're not there yet, Quinn," Larue said, puzzled when Quinn drew the car to a halt in front of the forested land that bordered the cemetery—and belonged to Trent Anderson.

"I don't want to get there," Quinn said. "Larue—I see a cop car in front—but I don't see a cop. I think we should move carefully. I want to get to Danni..."

His voice trailed. "Larue."

"What?"

"Look."

He pointed toward the woods right before them. A car—mangled like a tin can—had been pushed into the brush, and almost covered over with broken branches and high grasses.

"What the hell?" Larue said.

"That's Colleen's rental," Quinn said, his heart suddenly thundering at a frantic beat. "Something is happening now," he said, fighting for control.

He had to stay in control. His life could depend on it—and more importantly, Danni's life.

Danni is smart and strong. He knew it; he believed in her.

Wolf let out something between a bark and a howl.

Quinn opened his door and turned to the dog. "You've got to stay here right now; this is a quiet mission. Okay, stay, Wolf."

The dog looked at him unhappily, but obediently lay down, putting his nose between his paws as he stretched over the back seat and whined again quietly.

"Good boy," Quinn said. He turned to Larue. "Let's enter in a sideways motion and be ready."

"Quinn, we should call in—the girls might have been struck by a hit and run driver, or not a hit or run. Someone might have called an ambulance. They could be—"

"They're in the cemetery, Larue."

"There's a parish cop car—"

"And no cop," Quinn said. "Hey, please. I'm asking you to let me call this one my way."

Larue nodded.

They both exited the car quietly, slipping into the woods and moving through the trees, skirting the area of the broken stone wall.

They'd just reached a knotted high hammock area thick with cypress when Quinn paused, lifting a hand to Larue and pointing.

They'd found the cop. Looking past a one-winged angel, they could see him.

He'd been stretched out on top of a tomb.

Dead or alive, Quinn didn't know.

He moved silently, hopping over the broken wall, Larue behind him, as he hurried to the tomb, looking around.

They reached it.

Blood trickled from the cop's forehead as he lay, arms crossed over his chest, silent as death.

Quinn touched his throat.

He was still alive.

But is Danni still alive? And if so...

I sure as hell have to find her, fast.

***

The sound of the laughter came closer. Hunched down in the brush before the entrance to the first of the mound vaults, Danni kept as silent, barely breathing.

She felt torn and twisted.

John Appleby was on the ground in front of one of the scarecrow poles.

It was obviously meant for him, and there were two more.

Something twisted in her gut.

It just couldn't be Colleen—she simply couldn't be involved in this.

She had been in the car; she had been the driver. She had been coming out here, with or without Danni. She had known Danni, and long before Danni had taken over the *Cheshire Cat* and become a collector, she had believed a friend had to be helped, no matter what.

Colleen knew that about her.

Had she taken off like a bat out of hell, knowing that Danni would follow her? Had she somehow braced before the collision, and avoided being knocked unconscious?

John Appleby needed help, but Danni could hear the soft sound of laughter coming closer and closer.

Then the killer walked toward John Appleby, and paused by his side hunkering down.

"Ah, my dear wreck of a man!" she said. "You were wonderful. You served my purpose so very well. I am delighted I got to know you! But you must realize, really, that...you're not much of a man. You're barely surviving. Tonight...well, for you, tonight will surely be a mercy!" She stood, surveying the three scarecrow poles. "Don't worry, my friend. You won't be up on a pole. You'll be here, right down here on the ground, the bloody knife in your hand! You have to prove Trent Anderson is innocent, you see."

She stood straight and looked around, staring at the entrance to the tomb.

For a moment, Danni thought she'd been seen.

But the killer smiled, hunkering down again. "She'll be up there, though. Little Miss Perfect, with her flashing eyes and auburn hair and perfectly charming house and...Quinn. Mr. Perfect! Maybe he won't be so perfect when she isn't around, but he'll learn to live with it. Now, don't worry. I don't think anyone anywhere would believe you had gotten Quinn up on a pole. He's off in New Orleans. And the cop...ah, well, the cop...you already bashed him hard in the head. You disillusioned old man."

She was fingering something around her neck as she spoke.

The medallion, Danni thought. The real medallion.

"It's almost over," she said, rising again. "He'll be here soon. I never start without him. Together...well, soon enough, they'll know the man I want is innocent...and this whole thing was about love and happily-ever-after, right. You really never had a life. I doubt anyone will have a problem believing you killed yourself—after what you'd done! Disillusioned creepy old dude—it will all be over soon! He just needs time to get here...because I can't do it all on my own."

He needed time to get there. Who? Trent Anderson? Who else?

Danni weighed her position carefully; she didn't have anything on her. Not mace, not pepper spray...nothing. She also didn't have much time. If she could take down this half of the duo...

She was about five-ten and fairly muscular and active. She wasn't fond of fights, but Appleby and the cop who was lying somewhere might not have much time.

John Appleby hadn't moved—was he still alive?

She had to take a chance; she had to stop what was happening and reach Quinn or Larue or Ellsworth.

She tore out of her hiding place like a torpedo, and thankfully she did have the element of surprise.

And her surprise worked. She slammed into Tracy Willard hard, sending her flying down to the ground. Instinct must have been with her because she found a good-sized portion of a broken tombstone and cracked it down on Tracy's head, not trying to kill her, just immobilize her.

Tracy screamed, but with Danni straddled over her, she gave up the fight. She blinked furiously, trying to remain conscious.

They'd been quick to think of the killer as one man. A man—because of the strength needed for the poles, and to hike bodies up on them, and, of course, a man was involved.

Trent Anderson...

Obviously, he and Tracy could provide alibis for one another.

"Hey!" she heard a cry and while keeping a hand solidly on Tracy's chest to make sure she was in power, she turned.

She was stunned to see the man walking toward her at a leisurely pace.

Bearing a gun. A Sig Hauer, she thought.

What difference did it make?

"Nice job," he told Danni. "But if you will...get off her, please."

She stared at him, stunned. From his expression—pleased and superior—she knew instantly she had been wrong, so wrong.

Trent Anderson wasn't the killer.

Beneath her, Tracy began to laugh. "Oh, you thought Trent. Of course, you thought Trent! You silly, silly woman. Old John Appleby will be blamed—I could have Trent blamed. He's so rich and really, quite good in bed. I'm going to marry him, you see. Then I'll be so, so rich. There was no way I could allow him to see Belinda Cardigan again—or Ally! Ally didn't even want him, but she was getting in my way, and was seriously such a bitch. Now, this will be perfect. Our three of three. You, Colleen, and..." She paused, frowning, looking at her accomplice.

"Don't worry; I have it planned," he said.

"Get the hell off me! Lady," she shouted to Danni, "your time has come!" As she spoke, pushing Danni away, she flipped a pendant out from beneath her blouse and shoved it beneath Danni's nose.

"This, Miss Cafferty, this...it's the real deal! Just like magic—helping us get everything done! Helping us make the final sacrifice. Oh, that will be you, of course! I think I'll let you watch Colleen die. We do have a dug-up corpse?" she asked her accomplice.

"Don't worry—I have it planned," he said.

***

Quinn as flush to the ground as he could get was coming around small family mausoleums, tombstones, cherubs and weeping angels. Larue was heading toward the front, calling for help for the downed officer, and for major reinforcement.

He wasn't sure if he wanted dozens of cars coming with sirens blazing—the killer or killers might begin to feel desperate. Midnight, the witching hour, seemed to be the customary time for them to kill, but if he or they feared the law was closing in, desperation might alter the time frame.

When it came, the night came quickly. There were no lights in the cemetery that night; but as the night claimed the sky, a sliver of a moon began to rise casting a meager token of light.

He thought he heard something; a scream.

It was coming from just behind the three little tomb hills— where straw had replaced discarded bones in coffins.

He moved around the first of the hills as quietly as he could, staying low to the ground, and then going flat down upon it. He could hear someone at work there. It sounded like a hammering.

He crept closer.

There were three poles staked into the ground. In the weak moonlight, he could barely make them out—or the victims being strung up on then.

There was a body crumpled on the ground by the first— *John Appleby,* he thought—and there were three bodies on the poles. Living, as of this moment.

The first was Colleen Rankin who was either dead or knocked out. The second—alive and well and kicking—was Tracy Willard.

The last, where a man stood upon a small step ladder creating an elaborate tie on one of her arms while she kicked and squirmed, was Danni.

Fighting away, yes, that's my Danni.

But she wasn't the only one fighting.

Tracy Willard, strung up on the second pole, was shouting every manner of vitriol at the man.

It wasn't Trent Anderson, but it was the last man he had expected.

Though quite possibly, the first he should have.

"You slime! You are nothing without me. You are worthless—a computer nerd, no not even a nerd, a slob, an ugly slob. You need me, you have nothing without me, nothing!" Tracy shouted, her voice a cross between terror and tears.

Larry Blythe paused in his administrations to Danni and her pole, turning to Tracy. "You are a whore, selling out to the highest bidder. Who did everything—everything? All you wanted to do was kill. Who learned about the three scarecrows and sacrifices? Who had the straw delivered to Trent

Anderson's without him ever knowing? All so we could get away with this, and all the while I thought you meant for Trent Anderson to take the blame. But...all that. And you still treated me like—what was that you said? A computer slob. I did it for you, I did it all for you, and all you wanted was to snare that poor man, take him for everything, and move on. I wouldn't have gotten as much as a thank you. But—"

"I'm the one who has the medallion, the magic...our way to freedom!" Tracy cried.

Quinn knew he needed to make a move; he could see Larry Blythe's weapon was something like a large bowie knife, and it was sheathed in a leather case at his side. It must have been very sharp—he had slashed throats almost to the bone already.

He pulled his Glock, rising. Whether the medallion truly wielded a safety net for a killer or if instinct had kicked in for Larry, he swung around instantly sliding the knife from its sheath and placing it towards Danni's throat.

"Come out, come out now!" Larry cried.

Quinn stood and stepped forward, his Glock trained on Larry.

Larry just smiled.

"You know, you could shoot me, but this is a great blade. You'd never believe it, but I bought it from a honky-tonk place out here. Cleans up real nice, too. So throw that gun down now. Or watch her bleed."

"Shoot him! Shoot him!" Tracy screamed. "He's insane. He's the one who did all this. He's going to kill Danni, and Colleen...and me! It's him, he did this. Shoot him, shoot him, shoot him..."

The knife edged closer to Danni's throat.

Larue burst out of the bushes from the other side of the hill tombs, shouting.

"Drop it, Larry Blythe, do you hear me? Drop it!"

Quinn had maintained his Glock so far; he lifted a hand to Larue meeting Danni's eyes.

He almost smiled. She didn't appear to be afraid; she was looking at him with steadfast eyes.

"Quinn!"

She didn't cry out in fear or begging he drop the gun. She sounded almost as if they had met up at a mall, and she just needed to know what was going on.

"Your ankle...I thought you were limping. Does your ankle hurt?" Danni asked.

He knew, of course, what she was asking.

"My ankle is just fine," he said.

"Who give a rat's ass about his ankle?" Tracy demanded. "This maniac is going to kill everybody."

"Don't believe her! She knocked out the cop. She killed Belinda and Ally," Larry said, "but seriously, drop your weapons."

"Larue! Let's do as he asks!" Quinn said.

Larue hesitated. Quinn couldn't really see his friend's face in the minimal light of the pale moon. He had to hope he would trust him.

"Okay, get the knife away from Danni. I'm going to drop my gun down on the ground. See, I'm doing it right now."

"Push it far away from you, You, too, cop!" Larry called to Quinn and then Larue.

Larry gave them a huge smile as they did so, shaking his head.

"Stupid cops, they'll do it every time!"

He turned to Danni, smiling pleasantly, eyeing his knife with pleasure. "You know I got the gun, too. But if they try to rush me...oh, wait! I'm going to kill you now anyway!"

He should have taken greater care with Danni.

He hadn't secured her feet.

She gripped her "scarecrow's" wooden arms, using them for leverage, and she kicked him. Hard. Swearing and screaming, he went tumbling down backwards from his step stool, waving his knife continuing to spew his hatred at her he rose up, plunging back toward her.

By then Quinn had drawn his weapon from his ankle holster.

"Stop; I'll shoot!" he warned.

Larry didn't stop, he spun around, dropping the knife, reaching into his waistband for the gun he had there. He swung toward Danni again.

Quinn took aim, but he never got off his shot.

At that moment, it sounded as if a hound from hell had suddenly sent an echo through every tomb in the decaying cemetery.

Larry Blythe screamed, and even Tracy Willard, strung up to die, betrayed by her accomplice, let out a scream.

Wolf bounded over the last of a series of broken stones and took aim himself.

Larry Blythe never even got his gun up. The giant hybrid dog leaped atop him, dragging him down, a death grip on the hand that held the gun.

Quinn ran over and kicked the gun far from the man. Larue rushed forward then, securing the weapon, hurrying to check Colleen's condition, and bring her down from the pole.

For just a few seconds, Quinn stood over Larry.

He wasn't worried; Wolf had the man secure.

Larry Blythe looked up at Quinn, dazed.

He smiled. "We almost had it—perfect murders chalked up to legend for all time." He shook his head. "But. No fair," he said. "I didn't know I was going to be fighting a werewolf."

Quinn stepped past him, tall enough to stretch up and free Danni.

She looked down at him, and said, "I kicked butt at first, really. You would have been proud. I believe I gave Tracy a lovely black eye.'

He smiled at her pulling her into his arms.

"Did you get the medallion?"

"Still on Tracy."

"We'll get the damned thing, rip it to shreds, and see it can never be put back together again."

She slipped from her scarecrow-holding stake into his arms, holding close to him as she asked, "Quinn, do you think it was the medallion? Or just...someone who hated others and wanted an excuse for murder?"

"We'll never really know, will we?" he asked.

The sound of sirens burst all around them. Footsteps pounded across the terrain. Peter Ellsworth had come with his troops.

"Colleen?" she asked worriedly.

"She'll be okay," Larue shouted.

"I didn't do any of it!" Tracy screeched. "Whatever Danni says, it's a lie! It was him, Larry. He did it all, and—"

"Shut up, bitch! Your romance is over, baby. Your romance is all over!" Larry, still beneath Wolf's jurisdiction, said. And laughed.

Quinn drew back and slipped an arm around Danni's shoulder then called out to his dog. "It's okay now, Wolf. The policemen will get him. Time for us to go home."

Danni dipped down to embrace the dog. She looked at Quinn. "Home?"

"Home, God, yes, please! I can't take anymore vacation!

Epilogue

"You're lucky you were able to destroy the medallion," Father Ryan said. "What with all the police running around. If it was an antique, I'm sure there have to be a few local preservationists who must have wanted it set in a museum."

Father John Ryan, a good friend and most amazing priest, sat at the table in the kitchen at the house on Royal Street with Quinn and Wolf. The dog was seated at Quinn's feet, but he kept lifting his head to look toward the hallway to see if Danni was coming yet.

"We didn't give anyone a chance. As we got Tracy Willard down from her pole, Danni got her hands around the chain the medallion was hanging from. And—true or not true, we'll never really know—if you have no evil intentions or well of hatred in your heart, the medallion does nothing to you. Anyway, as soon as we were alone, I crushed the damned thing, burned it, made it fall apart—and then we buried it in about twenty pieces during our ride home. It's not coming back to life, and Tracy didn't even realize Danni had taken it when she did. Tracy Willard believed up until she was charged with first degree murder, she could shift the whole thing onto Larry Blythe."

"So, it was really her?" Father Ryan asked.

Quinn shrugged. "Tracy was apparently the one who found the medallion for sale at a little antique store off the highway.

She and Larry had both been out to the area several times, and they'd heard all the ghost stories. Once she had the locket in her hands...well, she didn't want any competition. And apparently, online and in person, Trent Anderson had shown interest in both Ally and Belinda—even though in life, from what I've heard, they were as different as night and day. Killing someone else to make it all look like a cult or local crazy meant nothing to either of them."

"So, jealousy and greed motivated Tracy Willard," Father Ryan said. "What made Larry Blythe get into it all?"

Quinn shook his head. "He saw all the beautiful women falling for just about every other man—and in his mind, acting like fools over other men for all the wrong reasons. Tracy was wearing the medallion that night, but she might have seen to it he had it at times? I don't know. Legends and stories are often somewhat true...but maybe not all be true to the bone. Sometimes events can come back and bite us. I have a feeling Yvette was murdered by her rival and not Percival's mother. I believe his mother was murdered before it could be proven she wasn't the killer. Not that I want to go back right away or anything, but somewhere along the line, maybe we could make a trip—and you could say a few words at that cemetery. Maybe let a few of the ghosts rest in peace."

"Of course, not that much of a drive," Father Ryan said.

Danni came into the kitchen. Wolf perked up and trotted over to her and she ducked down to embrace the dog as she said, "Not enough of a drive!"

"Ah, Danni, you can't blame an entire area!" Father Ryan said.

Danni shook her head. "I don't. I'm grateful for our outcome. We couldn't stop what happened before, but..." Danni paused. "I'm not sure the truth is all out yet, but I think Daphne Alain was intended as a victim, and they had originally planned their third 'three scarecrows' to be found at the harvest fairgrounds. I don't know everything, but those two did conspire to kill Belinda here—she was heading out to the event, and Tracy did not want her there. Here's the thing, both Tracy and Larry had access to all this information about so many people, because they had access to everything that was public on the dating site—and everything that was not. They were in New Orleans where Larry had found out about the mansion and the graveyard and because he was online constantly, and because they were both responsible for hospitality and for site inspections. What is so scary to me is the planning that went into what they did!"

"They identified the man killed with Belinda as a local. They must have targeted him because he was easy to attack," Father Ryan said. "But what about the man killed with Ally Caldwell?" Father Ryan asked.

"Again, easy enough for the two of them. Larry had hacked into all sorts of sites that had to do with Trent Anderson. He was supposed to be the scapegoat, as far as Larry was concerned. I think Larry believed until almost the bitter end Tracy would wind up with him. Somewhere in there, he must have figured out she was doing it all for Trent Anderson. I'll never really understand. But Detective Ellsworth was able to find out the man who drove Ally out was a local, someone who wanted to become involved with the lodge...and who was called and given the job of driving her out. No one at the limo company thought anything of him taking a car—or even that they hadn't seen him before. They were always hiring people. He had a record himself, which was why he was grateful to take the job when he got the call. We believe, one of the two—either Tracy or Larry—arranged for him to stop at the cemetery. It would be a gag to scare her—and he was probably told not to worry, it was being set up by Ally's boss," Danni said.

"Tracy was really the impetus—but it was easy to pull Larry into her snare. They killed four people because she wanted Trent Anderson. That must not be doing much for him," Father Ryan noted.

"Well, here's the oddest part of it all," Danni said, taking a seat and patting Wolf's head, where it now lay on her knee. "Trent Anderson and Colleen have been spending time together, trying to help the authorities find answers to many of the remaining questions. And...well, it seems they're going to be seeing more and more of each other."

"Ah, well, good for Colleen," Father Ryan said. He looked at the two of them. "And you don't seem to mind you lost your great vacation with the pool and the great room and the activities and all?"

"No!" They both said emphatically.

Father Ryan grinned and stood. "Well, I'd best be getting back to the rectory for the night. I'll see you two soon enough I suspect."

Quinn and Danni both rose to see him to the door.

When he was gone, Quinn turned to Danni.

"Are Billie and Bo Ray still setting up your Christmas ornaments? You were always such a big believer in not starting too early, in enjoying the fall, using..."

"Harvest decorations," she said.

He shrugged.

"Not this year!" she said. "I'm just ho, ho, ho, all the way!"

"Great. Well, hm. I've a little surprise for you then."

"You do?"

"Upstairs!"

He swept her up into his arms and made his way across the hall and to the stairs, hurrying up them and into their room on the second floor.

He pushed the door open and let her observe his efforts.

Delightful lights twinkled everywhere in shades of red and green. Elves sat on the mantle. A giant stuffed reindeer sat on the bed, and a small tree and a creche dominated her dressing table.

Danni smiled at him. "Ho, ho, ho!"

"Christmas all the way. Want an early present?"

"Oh, you're a present, are you?"

"Don't like to brag, but..."

Danni laughed. She squirmed out of his arms and over to the bed. The giant reindeer landed on the floor. He came down with her, and the lights continued to blink and sparkle soon casting their colors upon naked flesh.

He rose above her and told her softly, "You, my love, are the best present I've ever had in life, and I thank God you love me, too."

Later, she curled into his arms.

"You're not a bad gift yourself," she assured him. "Especially because..."

"Yes?"

"I don't think I ever, ever want to be on dating site!"

New York Times and USA Today bestselling author, Heather Graham, majored in theater arts at the University of South Florida. After a stint of several years in dinner theater, back-up vocals, and bartending, she stayed home after the birth of her third child and began to write. Her first book was with Dell, and since then, she has written over two hundred novels and novellas including category, suspense, historical romance, vampire fiction, time travel, occult, sci-fi, young adult, and Christmas family fare.

She is pleased to have been published in twenty-five languages. She has been honored with awards from booksellers and writers' organizations for excellence in her work, and she is the proud to be a recipient of the Silver Bullet from Thriller Writers and was awarded the prestigious Thriller Master Award in 2016. She is also a recipient of the Lifetime Achievement Award from RWA. Heather has had books selected for the Doubleday Book Club and the Literary Guild, and has been quoted, interviewed, or featured in such publications as The Nation, Redbook, Mystery Book Club, People and USA Today and appeared on many newscasts including Today, Entertainment Tonight and local television.

Heather loves travel and anything that has to do with the water, and is a certified scuba diver. She also loves ballroom dancing. Each year she hosts a Vampire Ball and Dinner theater raising money for the Pediatric Aids Society and in 2006 she hosted the first Writers for New Orleans Workshop to benefit the stricken Gulf Region. She is also the founder of "The Slush Pile Players," presenting something that's "almost like entertainment" for various conferences and benefits. Married since high school graduation and the mother of five, her greatest love in life remains her family, but she also believes her career has been an incredible gift, and she is grateful every day to be doing something that she loves so very much for a living.

Made in the USA
Lexington, KY
14 March 2019